FINALLY
in the rain

PRU SCHUYLER

For anyone that needs a hype girl to believe in them,
I will be yours.

Find Me in the Rain Playlist

Create this playlist and listen while you read for the full experience.

"River of Tears" by Alessia Cara
"The One That Got Away" by Brielle Von Hugel
"There Will Be a Way" by Dotan
"Robin Hood" by Anson Seabra
"Dear First Love" by LØLØ
"I Can't Make You Love Me" by Dave Thomas Junior
"Different Eyes" by Marco Tamimi
"I Found" by Amber Run
"Love Me Again" by Katelyn Tarver
"Train Wreck" by James Arthur
"Hold On" by Chord Overstreet
"Problems" by DeathbyRomy
"Harder Than the First Time" by Blake McGrath
(Theme song of *Find Me in the Rain*)
"Perfect" by Cole Norton

"Let Me Hurt" by Emily Rowed
"I Hate U, I Love U" by Kurt Hugo Schneider and Sam Tsui, featuring Madilyn Bailey
"Rebound" by Jenny March
"Coping [Explicit]" by Rosie Darling
"Before You Go" by Gracey
"WOW (Remix)" by Zara Larsson, featuring Sabrina Carpenter (I played this for every club and dancing scene.)
"Perfect" Covered by Madilyn Bailey
"I Saw You" by Jon Bryant
"I Miss You" by Grace Grundy
"Supermarket Flowers" by Ed Sheeran

PROLOGUE

SIX YEARS AGO

The stark white of the envelope in my hands reminds me of snow. Which makes me think of Alec all over again. Of skating behind Al's Barbecue, to touring Christmas lights in town, to falling in love. My breath freezes as I sigh. My cold fingers pull the mailbox door open, and I set the envelope inside.

Closing it back up, I turn on my heels and walk away from Alec's house. All air is ripped out of my lungs. Everything comes down to this letter. The puck's in his zone.

"Either way, we will be all right," I tell the little bean growing in my stomach.

And I walk away from the house. The house our baby boy will never step foot in.

*"We don't have time to prepare for the greatest moments;
they just simply find us when we need them most."*

"Hey, Char, will you just get me an iced mocha?" I ask her as I undo Jack's car seat.

"You got it." She spins and walks into Nikki's Coffee, her blonde hair flowing in the wind and Josh right on her heels.

Jack stirs, and I stop moving, watching him slowly come out of his nap. I can't believe that I made this little boy, he is the epitome of perfect. I brush his chocolate-colored waves out of his eyes as they flutter open.

"Where are we?" Jack's sweet voice sings in my ears.

Smiling at him, I say, "Getting coffee for a bit, and then we'll head home. Okay, bud?"

Yawning, he nods his head as I finish undoing his straps.

As if he wasn't sleeping moments ago, he hops down out of his car seat, grabbing his Paw Patrol backpack, and shouts, "I'll race you!" as he takes off for Charlotte.

I grin ear to ear and shut the car door, taking off after him. "You're going to lose!"

I let him get a nice lead, so he thinks he's winning, and then I take a few long strides to catch him, hooking my hands under his armpits and lifting him into the air like he's flying.

He erupts in giggles, and the couple walking past us beams at him. You just can't help it; his laughter is contagious.

I settle him down on my hip and step inside. Charlotte is already in our booth with our coffees and Jack's chocolate milk. She puts her phone down as we approach.

"Hey, big man. Have a nice nap?" Charlotte asks.

I set Jack down onto the booth, and he clambers right over, practically ripping his milk from her hand.

But before she lets go, she lifts her brows and says, "Manners."

He rolls his eyes with a full smile. "Chocolate milk, pleeeease."

Her resolve immediately fades, and she gives in.

Smiling, I slide into the booth next to him, and a wave of guilt hits me that I can feel happiness while my mom lies in a hospital bed.

My phone starts buzzing immediately, pulling me out of my thoughts. But I have a feeling I know who's calling, the same call I always get. I ignore it, not wanting to have the same conversation with the person on the other line that I have already had a thousand times. I down a couple of big gulps of my coffee and close my eyes, sighing.

Charlotte's hand covers my own, and I realize I might have sighed louder than I imagined, and she leans in to whisper to me. "You can't keep avoiding their calls. You'll regret it. It'll be okay, Lu." She squeezes my hand before returning it to her own cup.

The bills never end. I get one paid off with my tips, and then, *bam*, another one pushes me further into debt. I'm drowning, and I can't break the surface. My mind drifts as I watch Charlotte and Jack play with his toy dinosaurs that he dug out of his backpack.

I miss my mom so much. I know she's still here, but she's not at the same time. She can't smile, she can't laugh, she can't *live*.

With my mind still lost in the depths of my fears, I barely hear Josh join our table. He scoots in next to Charlotte, draping his arm over the back of the seat.

His eyes search mine, and his brows furrow. "Everything okay?"

I glance at my phone without even realizing it. "I—" I don't want to lie to him, and I don't really want to lie to myself. God knows I do it enough.

He sighs, and I'm guessing Charlotte told him more than she was supposed to. "It'll be okay."

"That's what I keep hearing." It comes out deadpan. I don't know what else to say.

The doctors avoid making eye contact with me when I visit. Either out of sadness for my mom's condition or sadness for my own. My visits used to be daily and then every other day. But the more she fades, the harder it is to see her. Now, I force myself to go at least once a week, on Sundays.

I haven't been able to sleep since she went into a coma, but it's gotten worse these last couple of weeks.

Jack is my only light right now. Of course Char and Josh, too, but it's different. I've been throwing myself into school and going through the motions at work. But living with Char and Josh helps me in more ways than one. With bills, with someone to watch Jack when I can't. I don't know where I'd be without them.

I refocus on what's actually in front of me and tune back in just in time to see them looking at me questioningly.

My word fumbles out. "What?"

Char's eyes soften, and I see the pity in the corners. "Don't, okay?"

Her head tilts in a silent plea, but I shake my head.

"Do you want me to watch him tonight? You guys should go do something," Josh offers.

Char instantly lights up, clasping her hands together. "Oh, please. Come on, Lu. When was the last time we had a girls' night? We could get all dressed up, maybe go out?"

It is tempting. I'm so busy with work, school, and Jack that I rarely make time for myself.

My lips just begin to lift into a smile when she launches herself at me over the table top, wrapping her arms tightly around my shoulders.

No backing out now.

I try to pry her death grip off of me, and she begins tickling me. I can't help the bubbling laughter that follows.

"Stop! Stop! Okay, you have me for two hours outside of the house. Then, I want to be back home and in bed. So, what's the plan?"

She ponders the question for a second, and I can see the wheels burning rubber in her mind.

She takes another second longer, considering what I imagine is a thousand ideas before it all spills out of her mouth. "Okay, I say, let's get all dolled up and check out that new bar on Fifth Avenue. Or we could go to Fireflies?"

Fireflies is a club downtown. It's always packed, and you have to wait for, like, an hour just to get in. But it's beautiful inside. The ceiling is covered in twinkly lights, which not only set the vibe, but are also gorgeous to look at. On top of that, the floor has built-in lights that react to your steps. And the staff always dresses up in themes. It's such a fun place. I've only been once, but it was one of the most fun nights I've ever had.

With my mind made up, I smile at her. "Fireflies."

She's the one who showed me the club in the first place, and it's her favorite way to spend a Saturday night.

Her smile stretches across her face, wrinkling her eyes. "Oh, thank God." She huffs a laugh out, clearly satisfied with my decision.

The arm of my shirt gets tugged twice. When I look down, Jack is leaning against me, an urgent plea in his eyes.

I lean in, whispering to him, "What's wrong?"

His big brown eyes suck me in. He sits up as tall as he can, pushing his lips against my ear. "Mom, I have to poop."

I can't help the giggle that escapes me. He's grown up around Char and Josh. He's known them since the day he was born. Yet he feels the need to whisper about going to the bathroom.

"Okay, come on, buddy. Let's go potty," I say as I slide out of my seat.

Little fingers grab ahold of my hand as I take my first step toward the restrooms. The smallest action that absolutely wrecks my heart. This boy has me, heart and soul, wrapped around his fingers.

We head into the women's empty restroom, and I help him get up onto the toilet.

He starts humming. It sounds familiar, but I can't place it.

"What are you singing?" I ask him.

He snickers. "Uncle Josh was playing it when he picked me up."

Oh no.

His humming continues, and a few moments later, the lightbulb burns so bright in my mind that it bursts.

My hand flies to his mouth, smothering the hums.

I'm going to kill Josh.

"Honey, you can't sing that song. That's an adult song."
Oh dear Lord, please don't sing that at school.

I don't care as much if he uses swear words when he gets a little older. But it's probably frowned upon in his classroom.

Those big puppy-dog brown eyes plead with me. "But, Mom, Uncle Josh lets me sing it!"

Are you kidding me?!

"We will talk to Uncle Josh after this. Are you done?"

I save my anger for Josh. Jack doesn't know any better.

"Yeah." He nods his head so sharply that I worry he'll get whiplash.

I grab some toilet paper and hand it to him. After he's done wiping, we get his pants re-situated and leave the restroom with my heart still beating too fast from my freak-out.

When our booth comes into sight, I can see some guy talking to Char, standing next to our table. And by the looks of it, she is enjoying every second. She's leaning forward on the table, her chin in her hand.

I finally catch a few words as we approach. "See you tonight then."

What?

Char notices me and turns her attention to Jack and me. "This is Laura and Jack. Laura's the one coming out with me tonight."

All right, Char, good for you.

His curly brown hair falls lightly on his forehead. And when his eyes meet mine, my breath catches. His eyes are so blue; they're mesmerizing.

"Hi, I'm Cam. Charlotte and I met in her class today. I'm really glad you're coming out tonight. Save a dance for me?"

Jack's tugging at my hand, probably wondering who this guy is.

"Yeah, sure," I mumble not quite sure how to flirt anymore.

His full lips tilt into a half-grin. "Good. I'll see you later, Laura." His body has turned to me completely.

"See you then," I mutter a little too eagerly.

His full-on smile reveals an almost-perfect set of white teeth. With that, he turns on his heels and heads out the door with his coffee.

I watch him leave, and Jack is practically shaking my arm like a toy at this point.

"Mom, who's that guy?" Jack jumps up into the booth next to Charlotte.

With no answer, I nod my head to her. "Char?"

After one last glance at him, she turns to me. "He and a few teammates came in today to promote their upcoming game. One of the players is from around here, I guess. He said the team will be there tonight. When I tell you that they could all fit in with the Hemsworth level of hotness, I am *not* kidding. Like, oh my God ..." Her voice trails off.

"Oh goody, a whole team of class-A Greek god D-bags." I roll my eyes.

Although she isn't wrong about at least one of them being crazy hot.

"I'm still going to dance with him tonight though." I laugh.

Might as well have some fun for my one outing a year.

Char and Josh toss their cups, and we make our way back to our car when I remember what happened in the restroom.

Once we are safe and sound and buckled up, I get out the DVD player for Jack to watch with the big headphones to drown out this conversation. Jack grabs my hand and holds it as his feet start to kick back and forth against Josh's seat.

Jack is singing along to *Frozen II* by the time we're five minutes into the drive.

With his attention elsewhere, I focus mine on the J boy up front behind the wheel. "Hey, Josh, question for you." My mom tone comes out without even trying.

He looks at me in the rearview mirror. "What's up?"

I cock my head to the side and squint my eyes. "Tell me why my son was humming the melody to 'Bloody Valentine' by Machine Gun Kelly when we were in the restroom earlier?"

His fists wring the steering wheel, and he offers an apologetic smile. "Hey, go easy on me. Jack never, *never* jams out with me. But sometime last month, it accidentally came on because of shuffling and whatever, and he just started dancing. So, I left it on." He bounces his gaze from the road to me in the mirror, waiting for my response.

Little liar. He's never been able to lie to me since we were kids.

"Only once?"

His lips twitch—his tell. "Welllll—"

"*Josh!*" I smack the headrest of his seat.

He just laughs. "He loves it! You should see him sing and dance to that song. You'd be playing it, too, if you knew how much of an MGK fan he is!" He tosses his phone to Char, who immediately laughs and scrolls through his music.

"Don't you dare, Charlotte!" I keep my mom voice in use.

"Oh, lighten up, Lu. He seriously does love it. Just once. Come on." She turns completely around in her seat, awaiting my decision.

Okay, but is it bad that a part of me really wants to see him do this?

Curiosity gets the best of me.

I roll my eyes. "Once. One time. That's it."

Char whips back around with a huge grin on her face.

I turn to Jack and lift the headphones off and pause the movie. "Hey, bud. Josh says he has a song to play for you."

His eyes instantly light up. But then dim back down. "B-but you said this is an adult song and I can't sing it."

My heart sinks. At the end of the day, if some song with a few swear words in it makes his eyes light up like that every time, then I don't really give a fuck if he wants to do it.

I cup his cheeks in my hands. "Go for it, buddy."

Char hits play, and the beginning notes flood and boom in the speakers.

Jack instantly starts bobbing his head in the chair. Josh is singing right along with him, and Char is recording it all on her phone. I guess this will be hilarious when he's older.

He sits up straight right before the words start and then follows right along with MGK.

They finish the rest of the song. I'll give it to him—for a five-year-old boy, he killed it. Just got to get a few more of the words down, and he'll be set.

After I put Jack down and say good night, I can't help thinking of my mom. If she were awake, she would've laughed so hard at his concert in the car. She was always strict with me as a kid about cursing. But she would pay Jack to run up to me and cuss, just to laugh.

I really miss how she brightens everyone's day.

She's going to pull out of this, right? She has to.

Knock, knock.

"Yeah?"

Char comes in and plops into bed next to me. "Shall we get ready for our night?" She lays her head on my shoulder, nudging me every two seconds, reminding me of Jack.

"Yeah. I don't have a dress though." Anxiety settles into my chest, and I just want to cancel all of tonight's plans if I can't find something I feel confident in.

I suddenly remember that the one club dress I do own, I lent out to a classmate of mine. She got drunk and puked all over it. And I definitely didn't want that back.

She rolls over, propping her chin in her hand. "Oh, don't you worry. You know I own too many." She hops out of the bed and offers me her hand.

She leads the way to her room and informs me that she will be doing my hair and makeup tonight. Just to make sure I look my best. It's a blow to the ego because, apparently, I can't do that myself.

Although she's not wrong.

We pass Jack's room, and I decide to sneak a peek at my sleeping angel. I crack his door open and laugh silently. His mouth is wide open, and there is a river of drool running down his hand.

Having him so young was definitely challenging, but I wouldn't trade it for the world. I take one last look at my baby boy and close the door.

Then, I let Charlotte pull me to her room to get ready.

She whips a bottle of vodka out of God knows where and pours two shots. "Here's to a night of fun, hot guys, and no regrets!"

Hot guys and *no regrets* don't usually go in the same sentence.

Char slaps my hand away from my hair as we inch forward in the never-ending line. "You look great. Stop fussing!"

I can't resist pulling my dress down once more, feeling like my ass cheeks are about to make an appearance every five seconds.

Charlotte took the pleasure of selecting our dresses. For herself, she picked out a black body-con and stiletto Calvin Klein heels. She paired it with a dark smoky eye and pulled her hair up into a high ponytail.

For me, she chose a gold satin slip dress that feels like luxury. Thank goodness I had my own pair of black heels to wear tonight, or I would have been stuck wearing the same worn-out Converse I wear almost every day. She did my makeup—a little too dark for my preference, but I let her have her fun with a dark brown smoky eye and bright red lips. My soft brown locks are loosely curled down my shoulders.

The line moves forward a little, and we continue to scoot closer to the entrance. Fireflies is packed tonight, as always. There's at least twenty people ahead of us, and we've already been waiting for over thirty minutes.

The music is getting louder as we approach. It's crazy how you just get accustomed to the music once you're inside. While outside though, I feel like I should cover my ears at times because it's so loud.

Char is rapidly typing into her phone, and she's biting down on one intense smile.

"What's *all that* for?" I circle the air in front of her face.

Her eyes shoot to me so fast that I worry she might strain those muscles.

She clutches her phone tight to her chest, which is rapidly rising and falling. "Um, so you remember Cam?"

I roll my eyes at her, wondering where this is going. "Yes."

She asked like I would have forgotten that smile. Every single person in Nikki's noticed him.

After another quick text, she focuses on me again. "So, Cam set me up with this guy on his team. His name is Reed. He has the biggest smile in his selfies and this way about him that makes you want to rip your clothes off but also want to take him to family dinner to show off." She closes her mouth when she realizes how crazy she sounds, and I laugh. "Anywaaay, Cam gave him my number, and we are going to meet up tonight. I don't know, Lu. We really just clicked, you know?"

"That's great, Char. I can't wait to meet him."

I suppress all the words I want to say, like, *Charlotte,* the one *isn't going to be some guy from some sports team who is here to promote his game. True love doesn't exist. Better you start accepting that now.*

I've given that speech to her one too many times. But she refuses to think that soul mates aren't real. She will always believe in true love and fairy tales. I guess maybe it isn't so bad for one of us to be an optimist in that department.

The line moves forward again, and now, we are only a handful of people from the entrance. Char's Prince Charming says they're already inside.

I stow my phone in my clutch. Trying to have some fun involves not checking my phone every five seconds, which is damn near impossible when I'm away from Jack.

"Next," the deep, booming voice of the bouncer calls to the last two people ahead of us.

14

He checks their IDs, and the other bouncer stamps their hands and pulls the door open. Music pours out, filling our ears. And they take off inside, eager to melt into the crowd.

We step up to the wall of a man and hand him our IDs. Which I don't think even matters. Because he looks at them for all of half a second before handing them back to us.

He waves us through, and the other bouncer stamps our hands and opens the door for us. Charlotte nudges me with her shoulder, and her eyes widen with a mischievous look. Music envelops us, and we welcome it, stepping into the chaos.

The first step inside feels like walking into a different world. The floor is digital. It reacts to your step, lighting up from the slightest pressure. It creates quite a light show throughout the whole club. On top of that, everyone is decked out in their best outfits, elevating the whole experience.

A waiter cuts us off, heading for a table. Straight blonde hair cascades over broad shoulders. Poking out of the impeccable locks are pointed ears. The theme for the staff tonight must be something related to fae.

Flashes of work pop into my mind, getting soaked from dropping a coffee cup, as I start to regret not applying here. This has to be the most fun place to work.

We try to make our way to the center of the floor, where the bar is, to get our first drink. Char must be texting Reed with how locked into her phone she is.

A guy bumps me with his shoulder, and I stumble back, almost losing Char. I reach out and hook my arm around hers to keep us together. This crowd is intense.

The circular bar sits in the center of the room, creating a circle of people around it. It's fun as long as you're not trying to cut through.

After a thousand, "Excuse me," and, "Please move," we finally manage to reach the barstools lining the counter.

The bartenders are working crazy fast, mixing, pouring, and serving. I have no idea how they keep up with all the orders.

A petite blonde girl hands a beer to the guy to my right and then focuses her attention on us.

She shouts over the music, but it barely reaches my ears, so I rely on reading her lips, "What can I get for you guys?"

Charlotte slides her card across the bar. "We'll start a tab with this, please. And check our bags. Can I just get a Long Island iced tea?" She turns to me. "And for you?"

I look back to the bartender, glancing down at her name tag—Stacy. "Can I get a Wonder Woman? The drink."

She abruptly nods, and with no hesitation, she is off to get our drinks. Char and I set our bags on the countertop, and when Stacy returns with our drinks, she checks our bags in and matches it with our phone numbers for pickup.

Char's phone lights up on the counter, and I see the name *Reed* with a little pink heart next to it.

Wow, that was fast. I can't help but chuckle to myself.

She reads it and leans as close to my ear as she can physically get. "He said he's at the bar. Oh God. Do I look okay?" She pulls away, patting the skirt of her dress and combing her fingers through her hair.

"Perfect!" I shout to her, giving her a thumbs-up. "You look like the most expensive stripper."

She giggles and smacks my shoulder.

I start to look around to see if I can spot those gorgeous brown curls from earlier. But the bartender is back with our drinks before I can get a good look.

Grabbing our cups and turning, we place our backs against the counter and begin scanning the crowd.

Something catches my attention in the corner of my eye— an aura of arrogance and sex appeal.

Cam and who I'm assuming is Reed are making their way over to us. Cam offers this big, goofy smile that I can't help but smile back at. He lifts his arm and waves to us. They close the distance between us rather fast. Everyone seems to move out of the way for, as Char would say, the six-foot Greek gods.

Cam doesn't stop feet away from me; not until he's inches from my face. He leans down, placing a small kiss on my cheek before moving to my ear. "You look incredible, Laura."

I'm not used to casual compliments, and a blush stretches over my cheeks.

He pulls away, and I mouth the words, *Thank you.*

Reed and Charlotte are being all cute and shy, meeting for the first time. But I will give it to her—they do have instant chemistry.

Cam leans against the bar next to me, pressing his shoulder gently into mine. I look up to him, and in the flashing lights, his jawline looks incredible.

He must feel my stare because his lips tip up, and he slowly turns to me. He nods his head at my drink. "What do you got in there? It looks crazy."

He's not wrong. It's one of the reasons I like this drink. It's vibrant blue with bright pink at the bottom. And when you swirl it, it blends into this gorgeous purple.

I clear my throat. "It's a Wonder Woman."

I've put about half of this down in the last five minutes. Mostly out of awkwardness. *What else am I supposed to do? Just stand here?*

I giggle with no clue as to what's funny. If there were a picture in the dictionary next to the word *lightweight*, it would be a picture of me.

Being a lightweight has a big pro. It's very cheap to get drunk. Con: I'm a drinker who totally falls for peer pressure. That means, I always go past my limit.

I finish the rest of my drink probably too fast. Cam offers his hand for my empty cup. And I let him take it. He tosses my cup into the trash.

He sways back over, stopping almost toe to toe with me. I drag my eyes over his fitted button-up shirt to his stark blue eyes.

My gaze drops to his lips without my command. Definitely signaling that the alcohol is starting to take effect.

His lips tip into a smirk, and he takes a step back, offering his hand to me. "So, how about that dance, Laura?"

I playfully roll my eyes and place my hand into his. Turning, I make a mental note of where Char is.

Wow, it must've really been love at first sight—or first slip of the tongue. Because I can't tell where Reed ends and she begins right now. I laugh and turn back around, letting Cam lead me onto the dance floor.

Into the abyss of grinding bodies I go.

Once he finds a spot he likes, he lightly places both hands on my hips, letting me move them as I begin swaying to the music.

My drink is really kicking in. Tingles have started dancing on my skin. I revel in the feeling and in the overwhelming sensations rushing through my body.

The beat is pounding in my eardrums. I swear I can feel it in my chest.

Cam's grip begins tightening on my hips, but I do not mind in the slightest. In fact, I wish his thumbs would dig in just a little harder. He pulls me into him, closing the space between us. The next sway of my hips rubs right in line with his. And with this napkin of a dress between us, I can feel *everything*. I can feel the tightness of his jeans, of the want building in his pants.

His hands begin trailing up my sides, sending shivers in their wake. They slowly run back down. But they stop halfway, and his hands wrap around my hips.

My body reacts to him before I even know what happens. In one swift move, he spins me, smashing my ass against the front of his jeans.

A little out of breath from the shock of that and a little from how much I like it, I stop swaying. But soon after, my body catches back up, right as my breaths begin to quicken.

I push back, grinding my hips into his, falling back into line with the music. His fingertips dig into my sides, harder and harder, and pulsing sensations vibrate out from his touch. This man knows what he's doing.

I throw my arm up and around his neck, pulling his head down to my ear, and he takes advantage of it. He slides his teeth over my earlobe, biting hard enough to make me whimper.

His deep voice overpowers the music in my ear. "You're so damn sexy, Laura. Fuck."

That should not have the effect on me that it does. I push my hips back a little harder in response.

I look up and see Char and Reed have joined us on the floor, still trying to morph their bodies into one.

The song ends, and we pull apart for the first time in what feels like forever. I turn around slowly, a little nervous to face him after we practically had sex a second ago. But his attention is on the group of guys that just walked up to us that I somehow missed due to my nerves. It must be some more of the team because Reed and Char are making their way over too.

Cam and some guy with curly, super-dark hair are talking, but I can't hear a word over the noise. After a minute or so, the group heads back the direction they came, and Cam turns to me.

He leans down, purposely placing his lips on my ear. He flicks his tongue against my ear before asking, "Hey, want to go hang in the lounge for a bit? Get out of this crowd? Charlotte and Reed are going."

I nod my head against his warm lips, feeling them move over my ear. He lightly runs his tongue along the edge, eliciting a moan that I wholeheartedly intended on keeping in my throat but it slipped past my parted lips.

He wraps his hand around mine and begins leading us through the sea of people toward the lounge doors.

They must've rented out a room for a bit because they aren't free. But they are so nice. Leather seats line the wall. There's a full bar, a TV, and whatever else you could really want for a break from the craziness on the floor.

We approach the doors, and I turn back to Charlotte, finding a beaming smile stretched on her face. I effortlessly smile back at her. I really am having fun tonight.

When we get to the room they rented, there's about ten other guys in here. But only three of them have girls with them.

It's a refreshing break from the booming noise on the dance floor. There's just background music playing in here. We find empty spots on one of the seats, and Cam orders a few drinks for us.

A guy with shoulder-long brown hair comes to sit near us. "Hey, Cam, who's this?" He nods to me.

Irritated that he couldn't ask me himself, I stick my hand out. "Hi, I'm Laura." *Were my words a little slurred, or was that just me?*

He takes my hand, holding for a second too long. "Nice to meet you, Laura. I'm Matt."

His piercing blue eyes drop to my chest, and I can't help the eye roll that slips free.

"Eyes up here, bud," I correct him, no slurred words.

He tilts his head to the side, whistling. "Ooh, feisty. I like that."

Cam sits up a little straighter, but he laughs before he says, "Matt, chill out. Stop trying to scare her off."

He clicks his tongue on his teeth. "Fine—for now. Nice to meet you, Laura." He then turns his attention back to some of the other guys.

Cam's hand playfully glides back and forth on my knee, giving me an odd sense of comfort. "Hey, there's a party at a hotel near here. Would you guys want to come?"

I look at Charlotte, who I can tell has already said yes. Because she's practically giving me puppy-dog eyes mixed with an *I'll kill you if you say no* face.

This is my one big night out, so might as well do it right.

I smile, turning back to Cam, whose eyes are locked on to my lips. "Okay, yeah, let's do it."

He meets my eyes for a moment before addressing his teammates. "Hey, you about ready to head out?"

One of the players with straight red hair answers, "Yeah, we're just waiting for Kos. He ran to piss."

Kos? My heart stops. *There's no way, right?*

I laugh to myself at the utter thought that it could be Alec.

And anyway, Kos could be this guy's full last name. Definitely not a nickname for Alec Kostelecky.

Cam stands up, and in my state of complete denial I join him, pushing all thoughts of my buried past away but falling short.

I can't shake what his stare used to feel like on my body, what his soft lips on mine used to lead to, how his hand wrapped around my throat while he thrust into me used to make me beg him for more. How he was the only man I've ever loved. And the only man who made me so angry that I was ready to kill.

Soon, the rest of the room is on their feet, impatiently waiting for this guy, who I am praying is not Alec.

The hair on my neck rises as I hear the door click open and shut behind me.

I begin to turn, ready to see if it's really him. Because there's no way in hell it could be *him*.

Right?

He would be an idiot to set foot in this town again, to come near me again. I pivot around, facing my fears.

I slam my eyes shut, scared to look.

Please don't be him.

Please don't be him.

Please don't be him.

I hear him mumble something, my eyes fly open, and all hope is lost.

The wind is knocked cold out of me as panic settles in my chest to remain hidden from him. I'm not confronting him, not after all of these years.

I spin to Cam, words falling from my lips without thought. "Look, I'm so sorry. I feel sick. I think I'm going to go home.

I'll call you." I turn and take off for the door without giving him a chance to respond.

Alec still hasn't noticed me yet as he's turned to a couple of guys, so I quietly step behind him, reaching for the door.

All of a sudden, he's pushed back into me. I stumble and lose my step. But warm, solid, familiar arms catch me, pulling me into a firm chest. I'm thrown back in time to the day we met, which was eerily similar to this.

His scent hits me, invading my senses in every way, with memories of our past overwhelming me.

Out of an old habit, I inhale deeply, bathing in the smell of him, of home.

But this isn't my home anymore, and it never will be again. He steadies me and pulls back, getting a full look at me for the first time.

If he had anything to drink tonight, he's completely sober now. His face drops, eyes boring into me.

"Lu? Is that really you?" His voice is so quiet that I barely hear it, but every word burns into my ears.

I'm frozen in his deep hazel gaze, locked in his arms. I want to run as fast as I can, but I also never want him to let go.

His voice grows louder, but it's soft, caressing my heart. "Laura?"

I can't do this. I can't see him. I can't—

Jerking out of his grasp, I bolt out of the door. I race down the hallway, hoping every turn I make will take me outside. I don't stop until I burst into the cold air, which stretches over every burning cell in my body.

Heels click behind me. I can tell it's Char before I even feel her grasp my shoulder.

"Are you okay? Oh my God, Laura, I had no idea. I swear. Just breathe. Come on. Let's go."

I can't find the words. I don't know if I will ever find them. What are the words for running into your ex-boyfriend? The only one you've ever loved. The only one you've ever wanted.

The only one who ever destroyed you. And the only one who ever will.

Tell me what words describe the feeling of seeing the father of your son for the first time in years, the first time since he left you and your son all alone.

I lean my head against the cold window the whole cab ride
home. Char occasionally pats my shoulder or rubs my knee.
But my mind isn't present. I am a teenager with no fears in
the world.

I never expected to see him again, never wanted to. He'd
just left with no note, no good-bye. He had taken all our hopes
and dreams with him and left me with nothing but dust and
misery.

But I had my mom. She helped as much as she could, but
we still struggled to make ends meet, living paycheck to
paycheck. After all, babies are expensive. She was a
hairdresser and a damn good one at that.

And I worked part-time at our local diner. Some days
were better than others. I helped with the bills, but my mom
insisted I put at least half into savings for school.

After taking a year off of school after graduation, Josh,
Charlotte, and I moved out of our parents' houses and into a
place of our own.

Charlotte is enrolled in school with me, and Josh works
remote doing data entry, so his schedule allows him to help
out so much with Jack.

With my mom in the hospital, they are my only solid
foundation. Well, they have been for most of my life. After

Alec left, I felt like I was all alone. But I had Charlotte, and a little while later, Josh joined.

My lips twitch up as I think of how Charlotte and I met.

One day, the popular girl in school, Tessa Thriller, called me a "four-eyed-slut" because her boyfriend had asked me for my number. Which I denied, by the way. And, well, Charlotte has always been one to stand up for others.

She punched Tessa right in the nose.

Josh turned our duo into a trio shortly after. One of our classmates was hitting on Charlotte and even touched her without her consent. Josh stepped in and beat the kids ass. He has been by our side ever since.

It was the three of us against the world. They were there when I found out that I was having a boy. They were also at the hospital when I gave birth to Jack.

They aren't just my friends; they're my family.

Seeing Alec again was a punch to the gut. These feelings and blocked-out emotions flooded back into me at once.

His scent was the key to the lock on my heart. When I breathed him in, everything came undone. All the years of built-up heartbreak and pain came loose.

The cab pulls up to our place, and Char tips the driver.

The house is silent when we walk through the front door. Josh must have gone to bed. I glance at the big clock in our living room. Holy crap, it's four in the morning. I have never stayed out this late in my entire life. I guess I was drunker than I previously thought.

I kick my heels off, and Charlotte follows suit. After I lock the door up behind us, my feet guide me upstairs as I ache to be in bed. Char follows me to my room, quietly closing the door behind her.

She walks to my bed and pats the spot next to her. "Okay, let me inside that brain of yours. You haven't said a word since we left Fireflies."

Taking one last deep breath, I open my mouth, but everything attacking my heart and soul can't make it past my lips. "I don't know, Char. I'm kind of still in shock."

I drag my sore feet over to the bed and flop down on my fluffy gray comforter. She leans back, rolling her head to face me.

"I had no idea he was on the team, I swear, Lu. I never would've met up with them if I had known. I'm sorry." Her hand falls over my shoulder, pulling me into a side hug. Her voice is muffled from my hair. "But you have to admit, he turned out quite nice-looking. A long-lost Hemsworth brother, if I've ever seen one." She chuckles.

I roll my eyes at her. I mean, she's not wrong. The last time I saw him, he was this scrawny teenage boy. But now, he's a pro hockey player. When he caught me, I could feel every hard line and curve of his body. I can't even imagine what he looks like under all those clothes now.

Not that that's ever going to happen. I'm not going to see him again anyway. Especially if I have a say in it.

But as hard as I try to push him out of my mind, he just won't leave. He always has been stubborn.

Not only did his body grow up, but his face did too. His hazel eyes seemed deeper than before. And his jawline? *Oh my God.*

I'm not blind, okay? I can agree that he's sexy as hell. But it doesn't change the fact that he already destroyed me once, and I can't feel that pain again—I won't.

This is why I don't leave my house. Too many people, too many potential bad situations. I'd rather just watch a movie with my Jack.

Charlotte pries herself from our hug and rises off the mattress. "All right, babe, I'm heading to bed. I love you, and you're a bad bitch—don't forget it."

With that, she shuts my light off and leaves me alone. I slowly sit and unzip my dress, changing into a loose T-shirt. I brush my teeth and wash my makeup off, wiping away the remnants of the night.

I'm just going to pretend that this never happened. I never ran into Alec. I never saw how tall he became or how strong. Nope, it was all simply a figment of my imagination, a dream.

Throwing the covers over me, I plug my phone in and close my eyes, begging sleep to pull me under.

The door creaks, waking me from my slumber. Little pitter-patters sound on the hardwood, and the corners of my mouth tip up. A perfect way to start the day.

Jack hops up onto the bed and joins me under the covers. I lift my arm up, and he slides in, cradling his head under my chin. Putting my arm back down, I cocoon us inside the blanket.

Minutes later, sleep drags me under again. And when I wake up, Jack hasn't moved. He's still tucked in my arms, sound asleep.

Bzzz. Bzzz. Bzzz. Bzzz.

Oh dammit. I never turned my phone back up last night.

I gently untuck my arm from Jack's body and reposition his head on the pillow. Reaching for my phone on my nightstand, I can see someone's trying to call me. But my eyes won't focus yet—they're too sleepy.

I pull my phone off my charger. It's Josh.

"He-hello?" I whisper, my voice scratchy.

Josh laughs on the other end. "Oh my God, are you still sleeping?"

I mentally smack the back of his head. "No. Technically, I'm awake. Jack, however, is sleeping right next to me."

"Okay, well, Char and I are on our way home with groceries. We picked you guys up breakfast. Figured you might need a little Sunday hangover cure," Josh says, and I can practically hear the full smile on his lips.

"I'm the luckiest girl in the world." He's right; my head is killing me. "What are you guys doing for the day?"

"Not much. Probably just hanging at the house. Is Jack going with you?" he asks.

"I don't know yet. I thought I'd ask him when he woke up."

I instinctually glance his way. His chest rises and falls gently, calmly. Nothing compares to the peaceful look on a sleeping child's face. No worry, no concern, no fear. Innocence. Something I miss dearly.

"All right, I'm going to get him up. See you soon."

I end the call and place the phone back on the nightstand.

Giggles fall past my lips from the massive yawn coming out of his tiny self. When I roll over, big brown eyes peer back at me.

"Good morning, honey." I brush the brown hair out of his eyes.

"Morning, Mom." He yawns again.

"Come on, buddy. Josh and Char are bringing us breakfast." I run my fingers through his hair. "After we eat, I'm going to visit Grandma. Do you want to come?" I have a hard time meeting his eyes, so I throw the blanket off me and start picking out my outfit for the day from my closet as he ponders his answer.

I hear him land on the floor.

"Yeah, I miss Grandma. I want to tell her about my new toy I got last week. She's going to like it."

My gaze locks on to him, and I wonder how in the hell I got lucky enough to be his mom.

"Okay, bud, go pick out some clothes, and I'll meet you downstairs." With my outfit in hand, I head into the bathroom.

Jack takes off, almost running out of the room. I'll never understand kids' energy. I wish they could bottle it up and sell it, and then I wouldn't need so much caffeine.

After brushing my teeth and washing my face, I change into a pair of black jeans with a cream camisole and a pink cardigan.

I step into the hallway. My slippers feel like clouds on the hardwood.

Near Jack's room, which is right next door, I ask, "Jack, are you dressed?"

Crash!

Something shatters downstairs, and I take off before I even realize it.

I fly down the stairs, my heart pounding, as I run horrible what-if scenarios in my head. I bolt down the last few steps, heading straight for the kitchen. "Jack, are you okay? What happened?"

I turn the corner, preparing myself for blood and hours in the ER. Thankfully, neither of those has to happen. Two mugs have seen their last day, lying in pieces scattered on the floor. And Jack is standing safely on the counter with a chair pushed up against it.

His eyes are as wide as they can get as he waits for me to say something, his mouth quivering.

I take a step toward him. "Are you okay? What happened?" I walk closer to him with my slippers on, avoiding the chunks of sharp ceramic.

I reach my arms out to him, and his hands grip mine. I lift him off the counter, resting him on my hip.

He says in the most heart-wrenching tone, "I'm sorry, Mom. I was trying to get a mug down for you for your coffee."

My heart clenches.

When I found out I was pregnant, I was terrified. I was scared out of my mind to raise a baby, to help him grow into his own person. To be responsible for another human being. But moments like this make every sacrifice, every scary moment, one hundred percent worth it. Being his mom is the best thing I've ever done.

I set him down on the couch and take his cheeks in my hands. "That is so very sweet of you, buddy, but you could've gotten hurt. And I'd much rather have an unharmed you than a cup of coffee."

He smiles, but I can tell he's still a little shaken up. The front door opens, and Josh and Charlotte make their way in with their first round of groceries.

"Why don't you go help them carry stuff in? I'll get the kitchen cleaned up." I lean down, kissing his forehead.

He nods, and I lower him to the ground.

It dawns on me that I never noticed his outfit. His cape is whipping behind him. No wonder he was feeling a little fearless this morning.

He's Superman.

After we got all of the groceries put away and finished breakfast, we got ready to go see Mom. It's only about a ten-minute drive from the house.

We like to go see her every Sunday. We tell her all about our week, what happened, good and bad. I like to think she can still hear us. That when she wakes up, she won't skip a beat; she'll be up to date on everything in our lives.

I don't exactly remember when this became our new normal. When talking to her in a hospital bed became our routine. Instead of feeling her arms wrap around us, instead of feeling the warmth of her, when we hug her, we feel the cords and tubes surrounding her frail body.

I try not to focus on the sadness of it all, to separate my mind and my heart. But it's hard. It's hard to talk to her and not hear her sweet voice chime in or to say good-bye and not be completely enveloped in a warm hug. I never realized how much I took that for granted. I took it all for granted.

But I guess that's how it feels with everything in life. What's the saying? *You never know what you have until it's gone.* Something like that.

We pull into the parking lot and find the guest parking. By now, I do it out of habit.

Jack's fussing to get out of his seat. "Mom, hurry up! I want to see Grandma."

I undo my seat belt, falling into the motions of our visit. I open his door, and he practically jumps out the second he can. He grabs hold of my hand and all but drags me to the building.

Do you know the feeling when you're so full of emotion that you just go numb? Yeah, well, that's me every Sunday. My brain somehow compartmentalizes anything to do with my mom.

I haven't cried once since her stroke. I haven't shed one tear. I don't get it. I am usually so emotional over everything. The last episode in a TV series, the end of almost every movie, sad videos, all of it. But inside, I'm shredded to pieces, waiting for her to put me back together.

Once we get inside the hospital, we step onto the elevator and Jack presses the button to her floor. The elevator opens, and we head right to her room, smiling at Angie, one of the nurses who works here. She always goes out of her way to make all of us comfortable and content. I'm glad she's here, watching over my mom.

Seeing her in the bed, unconscious, never gets easier. It takes my breath. It doesn't faze Jack though. He runs up, hopping right onto her bed, snuggling into her side. Maybe it's because he's young. He doesn't know that this isn't normal, that most kids don't visit their grandma in a hospital bed on Sundays. But it's what he's known for a while, and he doesn't question it.

His words are tumbling out of his mouth so fast that they seem to merge together as he begins telling her everything. "So, Mom took me to get this super-awesome Superman costume, the one I have on. I know you can't see it, but it's the coolest thing ever. It has a cape and everything. I wear it all the time, even to sleep. I can't wait to show you. Maybe Mom could get you one, too, and then we could match. My week was okay. School's good. My friends are good. I want them to come here to meet you. But we don't really hang out much outside of school."

Seeing them together helps me forget all about the Alec incident last night. And I haven't decided if I'm going to tell her about that quite yet.

I find my usual seat in the chair next to her bed. Jack continues to go on and on. He tells her all about the TV shows he watched and how I let him cuss and sing that song.

Thanks for that, bud.

I know when she wakes up, she'll scold me for that but laugh about it afterward.

Jack is fairly quiet, but I swear he saves all of his words for her.

After about thirty straight storytelling minutes from Jack, Angie comes in and offers to take him to get a snack.

This is our usual routine. She does it, so I can have some alone time with my mom. I'm grateful.

Scooting my chair closer, I take her limp, cool hand in mine. "How are you doing, Mom?"

I wait for her to respond, praying to hear her voice again. Nothing comes.

I sit there in silence for a moment, contemplating what to say. But the only words that come out are, "So, I, uh … I ran into Alec last night." Hoping that will shock her into consciousness, I give her a moment before continuing, "We didn't really talk. He recognized me, and I … well, I bolted. I don't want to see him, Mom, but …" I trail off.

She's kind of become my diary through all this.

She's who I bare my soul to.

So, I speak freely, fearlessly. "But seeing him again, Mom … oh God. It was like all these locked-away feelings came back at once. It was overbearing. I should hate him, right? I should hate him for leaving me, for leaving Jack. I mean, I do … to a certain extent. But I feel like I should hate him more, you know? Anyway, I guess it's not that important because I won't be seeing him again."

I ramble on for what feels like hours. I fill her in on all of my classes and anything and everything from the last week. After a while, I snuggle into her shoulder. My body aches from the desire of wanting to be held by her.

After I finish talking, we just lie there in silence. My eyes drift. Being as close to my mom's embrace as I can get feels a lot like coming home.

Taking some deep breaths, I try to get any scent of her I can. But after months in the hospital, it's almost gone, replaced by the stale air from this place.

The door creaks softly, forcing my eyes open. Jack comes skipping in with chocolate on his lips.

Angie smiles at me, but I can see the pity in her eyes.

I sit up and grab my bag, ready to head home. I wish I could take her with me. "You ready, buddy?"

He smiles that too-big-for-his-face smile, showing chocolate bits on his teeth.

Oh goodness, what am I going to do with him?

"Yeah, can we stop for ice cream?"

I shake my head at him, suppressing a laugh. "You just had chocolate—or at least what made it into your mouth." I scoot him toward the door.

He halts, slamming his foot on the ground. Twisting around, he juts a finger at me. "There is no such thing as too much chocolate, Mom. Come on!"

Well, I'll give myself some credit. I surely raised him right. "Okay, fine. One scoop each and then home."

With the win in his pocket, he turns back around, chin high, and heads to the elevator.

Angie walks with us, a heaviness in the air between us. She's the first to speak. "It was good to see you guys. Next Sunday?"

I don't meet her eyes. "Yeah, next Sunday. Let me know if there are any changes."

She rests her hand on my shoulder. "Of course." Turning her attention to Jack, she says, "You be good for your mom, okay?"

Jack is bouncing up and down on his toes, begging me to hit the button so we can go get his ice cream. I hit it as he says, "Yeah, yeah. Okay, I will be. Bye, Angie. We have to go. Important things to do."

The doors glide open, and we step inside, turning to see a smiling Angie. We wave to her and then head down to our car, surrounded by the thick silence of sorrow.

Part of me can't believe it's only been a year since her stroke. But at the same time, it feels like it's been longer since she held me, maybe even forever.

The doctors said they don't know when she'll recover. That she should have months ago and they don't understand it. Just a phenomenon, I guess.

Her brain activity is normal and steady, but she just won't wake up. They say some parts of her brain might be damaged from the stroke. We lost her for a little bit, and she had to be resuscitated.

We won't know what the damage really is until she comes back to us. And we don't even know when that will be or if it will ever come. It's frustrating, and I … ugh, I want my mom back.

We drive to the little ice cream shop on the corner of our street, parking in the near-empty lot. I hastily get Jack out of his seat. He's practically vibrating from excitement.

The second his feet touch the ground, he's off, racing for the door. Again, I wish I could have an ounce of his energy. Right before he gets there, the door opens, and a familiar guy walks out.

Ugh.

Cam's head tilts with that stupid side smile. Two other guys are with him, but I don't think I recognize them from Fireflies.

I frantically look around, trying to see if Alec is with them. But unless he's still inside, in the restroom or something, he's not here.

Jack steps around them and heads inside, running straight to the counter. I can see him the whole time, and there's no onc else inside besides Rebecca, the owner, who I used to go to school with and trust. So, he's safe.

Cam speaks first, that deep voice cutting through the tension. "Hey. How are you?"

I rock back and forth on my heels. "Good. Just out for some ice cream."

He looks inside to Jack, and it hits me. *Does he know he's Alec's? Does he know anything about our past?*

Better to leave that stone unturned.

"Your brother is adorable. He looks a lot like you," Cam says with eyes of adoration.

I feel all the relief in the world, and a nervous chuckle leaves me. *If only he really knew.* I guess Alec has kept us a dirty little secret.

"Yeah, thanks. I should get in there before he orders the whole store."

He laughs a real laugh. "Hey, how do you know Kostelecky, by the way?"

My heart drops at the mention of his last name, a name I used to doodle in notebooks for hours. "Alec? W-we knew each other as kids." Nope, Cam isn't getting anything more than that. I end the conversation with, "Anyway, good seeing you."

He opens his mouth, but I leave no room for commentary and step around them, going inside and meeting up with Jack at the counter.

Rebecca is handing him samples left and right. At this rate, we won't even need to order anything. I glance back outside, but no one's there. The black Audi is pulling out of the lot, taking some of my anxiety with them.

I slam my door shut and take off for Harnet Hall. I have two minutes to get my butt in my seat, or I'm going to be late. Most professors don't care if you're late, but Mrs. Randall locks the classroom door at 10:01 a.m., if you're lucky. Most times, it's locked by 10 a.m., when class begins.

My alarm was supposed to wake me up at eight thirty, so I could get Jack ready and get him to school. Then get me to school. But that did not go as planned.

I woke up at nine and had a missed call from my boss to stop in today when I have a chance. Which put a bad taste in my mouth as she has never made such a weird request. I skipped makeup, my hair went into a high ponytail, and I threw a hoodie over the bralette I had fallen asleep in along with some leggings. I even let Jack wear his Superman costume to school this morning—that was how behind we were.

He ended up being about forty minutes late to school. Mom of the Year award goes to me.

Then, with my nerves eating me alive, I drove to work. My boss told me that they were closing, that business hasn't been good, and they can't afford to stay afloat any longer.

I'm glad I didn't put that conversation off, but dear god if that didn't add a world's weight of anxiety onto my chest.

I drove all across town to campus and found the closest spot to Harnet Hall I could, which, of course, was like a five-minute walk to my class since all the lots were packed.

I turn on the sidewalk that leads up the stairs and quickly close the distance to the double doors. A couple of students bustle out of them before I can reach for the handle. Pushing past them, I bolt for the staircase.

Second floor, room 215.

I hit the second landing.

Ten feet.

Rushing the last few feet, I throw my arm out, managing to get my hand on the door handle seconds before Mrs. Randall reaches for it from the other side.

I throw the door open and politely smile at her.

She raises one eyebrow. "Pushing it, aren't we? Find a seat, please."

I brush past her and sit in the closest seat I can find, practically top row—my least favorite spot. But it will have to do for today.

Setting my backpack on the ground, I unzip it, rifling through it for my notebook and pencil. Mrs. Randall locks the door and descends the steps to the front of the room.

I finally take a deep breath and settle into my seat. Tearing my gaze from my notebook, I look to the front of the room.

You have got to be fucking kidding me.

Nope, not today.

Not abso-fucking-lutely not.

I've dealt with enough, and it's only ten a.m.

I throw my notebook and pencil back in my backpack and zip it shut.

I stand up and throw my bag over my shoulder as I shuffle out of the row.

My hand is barely on the door when Mrs. Randall clears her throat in the mic. I roll my eyes and turn around. Everyone's looking at me and my cheeks flush a deep crimson.

When I let my gaze stray to the reason for my leaving, his eyes find mine instantly, and I can see the thousand questions he wants to ask floating behind his stare. But that's a rabbit hole I will not be falling down.

"Ms. Young, where are you going? Late to class and then trying to leave a minute in? Enlighten us all." Mrs. Randall locks her focus on me, awaiting my answer.

Are you kidding me right now?

I know I'm not every teacher's favorite student, but is this *really* necessary?

I put no amount of effort into my vastly vague answer. "I'm sorry. I have to go."

Mrs. Randall clears her throat once more. "Leave now, and you'll receive an F on the pop quiz today, which is fifteen percent of your grade. Please sit and be respectful of our guests." She smirks, knowing I can't afford that F.

Dammit!

As much as I want to wave my middle finger to the front of the class and take the F, I can't.

Sighing heavily, I drag myself back to my seat. I can't help my eyes from drifting to Alec and his team. He can't hide the little smirk on his face.

Annoyed, tired, hungry, and coffee-less, I sink into my seat, crossing my arms.

Mrs. Randall gives a brief introduction of the team and what they will be speaking about. They weren't originally scheduled for my class, so I thought I didn't have to worry about it. But the class they were supposed to be at got canceled at the last minute, so they came here.

Yay me.

One of the younger-looking teammates hands out a flyer to each of us for an upcoming game. I briefly glance at it, only out of pure adoration for the design and setup of the flyer. Whoever designed this knew exactly what they were doing. The bright black and teal combo is perfect, and you can't resist looking at it.

At the top are their team name and mascot facing off with the other team's mascot.

The New York Nighthawks take on the Minnesota Mystics.
ONE NIGHT ONLY!

They have the starting roster listed, and to no surprise, Alec's name made the list. Starting center, number 16.

My heart constricts when I see his name on the flyer. It feels like a lifetime ago that I was going to his high school games, cheering him on. And now, he's playing for the NY Nighthawks in the NHL. I'm proud of him and the life he has built for himself. I just wish sometimes that he had brought us with him. Instead of leaving us behind to pursue his dreams.

But that's not the reality. The reality is that he left us. He left pregnant me—and therefore adorable little Jack—to go play hockey. And that I can't forgive and never will.

Some of the players speak on how they set their goals and how they achieved them. So exciting, thrilling even. But this is an advanced marketing class, not some class with kids who need heroes and goals to pursue.

We all have our goals and dreams. Everyone in this class is a senior, not a freshman. Our dreams are already almost realized.

Number 33 finishes talking about the upcoming game and what to look forward to. The Minnesota Mystics went undefeated last season. Well, until they played the New York Nighthawks for the Stanley Cup and the Nighthawks won.

He passes the mic to Alec, and I try to keep my eyes anywhere but on him. But the second his deep voice fills the speakers, my gaze is forced up to his. I have no control.

"As you know, my team and I are touring our hometowns right now. And this town is mine. It's weird, being back here, all these old memories and old feelings." His eyes never leave mine. "It's like I've stepped back in time." He lightly laughs, and then his sincere gaze settles into mine. "I feel like maybe

I should grab my skates and go find that little pond back behind Al's Barbecue."

My heart drops to my stomach, and I suck in a breath that gets caught in my throat.

I almost forgot all about that little pond. We used to go there every single day. All of our free time together was spent at that pond. Skating, dancing, *living*.

So many memories flood my mind and vision, overwhelming me. We had our first kiss there. He taught me how to skate there. We fell in love there. And when he left, I never returned.

After a moment longer of looking at me with his nostalgic stare, he begins speaking again. "This is where I grew up, where I fell in love with hockey. Duluth was my home for most of my life. The Duluth Greyhounds was where I discovered my passion and drive. I owe this town everything I have." His eyes never waver from mine. "It would be amazing to have all my hometown's support at the upcoming game against the Mystics. *All* of you." He pauses, his hazel eyes searching mine.

But it's my turn to let him down. Because there is no way in hell I will be attending that game.

He passes the mic back to Mrs. Randall.

"Let's give a round of applause to our speakers today."

All the students clap enthusiastically, all the girls showing a sudden passion for hockey.

"Your pop quiz is on Blackboard, and it is due at eight p.m. tonight, no exceptions. Class dismissed."

Okay, hold up. I stayed to take a pop quiz, which I didn't even need to be here for! *Ugh!*

I grab my bag and storm off, cutting off everyone in front of me.

"Laura, wait!" Alec calls after me, which only makes my legs move faster.

I bolt out of the door and take off for the elevator instead of the stairs since it's closer. I hit the button, and it instantly opens, empty.

Thank God.

I step inside and smash my finger into the button to close the doors. It finally dings and begins sliding shut.

"Come on!" I shout at it, trying to speed it up. "Come on, come on, come on!"

It's two inches from closing when a hand slides in place, opening the doors back up. Standing outside of them is none other than Alec.

He's out of breath from chasing me. I'm a little winded myself.

That annoyingly stupid, beautiful smile of his is stretched across his face. "You always were able to outrun me."

He steps inside, and the elevator doors shut at a much faster pace this time around.

Thanks, universe.

"Which floor?" he asks.

I keep my eyes locked on the stainless steel doors. "One." My tone is harsh.

He presses the first-floor button, and the elevator shifts into gear, slowly lowering us down. He turns to me, giving me his full attention. "How are you? How have you been?"

I take a deep breath to try to steady my rapidly beating heart. But it doesn't work. At first, a part of me wanted to turn to him, let him hold me.

But now, I'm just pissed off.

Who does he think he is?

Anger floods my veins, boiling my blood.

This is what he says to me years later?

Years after he left Jack and me alone. Visions of Jack's birthdays and holidays flash in my mind. Of him opening his Christmas and birthday presents and hunting Easter eggs. Images of my mom in her hospital bed burn into my eyes.

And I go *rabid.*

I turn to him and shove his shoulders hard, over and over, until he hits the wall of the elevator. His eyes widen as he's taken aback by my physical response. They open so wide that they remind me of Jack's, which only makes me madder.

My eyes find his, daggers in my stare. My words fly out, too personal and too vulnerable, ones that I will certainly regret. "You want to know how I'm doing, *Alec*? How I'm really doing?" I push his chest. "Let me tell you. Well, for starters, my mom's in a coma. Has been for a while now. She is cold and so pale; she looks like she shouldn't even be alive. She should be here with me, with us. I'm drowning in her bills, and they never stop coming. On top of that, I'm recently unemployed. So, now, I'm stressed out about paying for school, paying for my mom's stuff, and paying for me."

I leave Jack out. He has no claim on my little boy.

"And now, Mr. Knight in Shining Armor comes waltzing back into my life, asking how I'm doing. Who I haven't seen in years, mind you. So, Alec, I'm doing just great! How about you?" I cross my arms over my chest and take a deep breath, feeling a little flustered from oversharing.

His crossed arms slowly lower, and he has to put effort into not touching me because of my closeness. I didn't even realize I had gotten so close to him when I was talking—or rather yelling.

I stutter-step backward, putting some space between us. But I can't ignore the tingles crawling on my skin from his contact. Even after all these years, he still has some magical effect on me.

His hazel eyes search mine, looking for something to grab on to. When he speaks, his voice is faint, full of pain. If only I cared. "Lu, I'm so sorry. I had no idea. Is there anything I can do?"

He reaches for my arm to give me comfort. But I pull away.

My eyes focus on the floor until the elevator door dings, opening to the sea of students moving between classes.

"No, Alec, there's nothing you can do." I turn to walk away but not before adding, "Actually, you can leave. That would make my life a hell of a lot easier." I huff.

As the words come out of my mouth, pain erupts in my chest. I'm shell-shocked, being this close to him after all this time. I want to turn to him, run into the arms of the only person who has ever felt like home. But Jack deserves better than that. *I* deserve better than to chase a guy who abandoned me when I needed him most.

I step out of the elevator, and he doesn't follow. I walk as fast as I can to my car, slamming the door once I slide into my seat.

Starting the engine, I'm frozen, unable to move. My eyes can't stay still, bouncing between my steering wheel and my white knuckles. The floodgates on my heart break, and locked-away pain and sorrow pour down my cheeks, staining my shirt and my soul. But I don't shed a tear for Alec, for my mom, I can't. Because once I start, I genuinely don't know if I will ever be able to stop.

"Take my hand, Clumsy." Alec laughs as I almost fall on my ass.

With my heart in my throat, I place my hand in his as he continues to try to teach me how to skate.

"There you go," Alec reassures me as I barely stay on my feet, skating shakily from my left foot to my right and back.

Alec's hands loosen their grip, and worry fills my body. I am totally going to fall.

But when his hands release mine, I stay upright, slowly skating by myself across the ice.

Alec jumps in the air, spinning around. Which made my *staying upright* skating feel a little talentless. "You did it! You're doing it! Keep going!"

I can't help the giant smile from breaking onto my lips and the blush that creeps up my cheeks. "I'm doing it. Oh my God! Oh my God, I'm doing it!"

I look away from Alec for one second, glancing down at my feet. When I look back up, Alec is standing right in front of me, and I immediately panic.

I throw my hands up to try to find some balance, but it is far too late for that. My weight shifts, and my legs fly out from under me. My ass smacks the ice, hard … right in front of Alec.

He immediately falls to his knees, and his eyes scan me, searching for injuries. But unless his stare is glued on my ass or my pride, he won't find any.

"Are you okay?" he asks.

I look up and notice that in the corners of his eyes, a wrinkle of humor lingers. And I can't help but laugh with him—at myself really.

The laughs burst from me, and I can't stop it or stop the ice that's melting and soaking through my leggings.

Alec stands up, as if that isn't a feat of its own. He offers me both of his hands, which I happily take.

He pulls me up, and my skates glide toward him, our lips only inches apart.

His eyes drop without hesitation, and I want nothing more than for our lips to touch, to kiss for the first time.

As if he reads my mind, my wish is granted.

Alec's hands slide around my lower back, securing me in place against his chest. And he closes the inches between our lips tortuously slow.

I've seen people kiss before, and I've imagined what this would be like—to have my first kiss. But all the times I have imagined it before is nothing compared to this.

Sparks explode from our lips when they collide. And I swear a flash of light goes off behind my eyelids.

We stay like that, locked in our kiss, and I know in that moment that I'll never want anyone else.

Only Alec. Only ever Alec.

As we pull away he whispers against my lips, "There's a letter from me in your mailbox, read it when you're alone tonight, Lu?"

Still stunned from our kiss, it takes me a moment to realize that he hand wrote me a letter.

Excitement thrums through my chest as I whisper back, "Of course."

"**G**rab the popcorn!" I shout at Josh, who's in the kitchen, as I wiggle in between Charlotte and Jack.

We try to have a movie night once a week, where we all get together. We pig out with snacks, drinks, the whole works. But we have been fairly miserable at keeping to the once-a-week plan. This is our first one in, like, a month.

We typically just throw out movie ideas until we all somewhat come to an agreement. But nine times out of ten, we always pick some action or comedy movie. And tonight is no different. We're watching *My Spy*, starring Dave Bautista and Chloe Coleman.

The opening credits are starting to play when Josh walks into the living room, finding a spot by himself on the love seat.

I lean over and yank the popcorn bowl out of his lap.

"Hey!" He throws his hands up in protest but doesn't ask for it back.

Jack and Char shove their hands into the bowl, grabbing fistfuls before I'm even settled back into my spot.

"Stop that!" I lightly slap their full hands away, giggling.

The opening scene begins, and we all hush up, focused on the TV screen in front of us. But shortly after, my gaze drifts to the little boy at my side and then to my two best friends.

How did I get so lucky to have these amazing people in my life? To have a bright son who loves life and laughs constantly. To have best friends who would do anything and everything for me at the drop of a hat. The only thing that could make this better is if my mom were here.

My thoughts continue to drift, finding Alec and my conversation with him earlier. How could he even have the audacity to talk to me after all these years? And on top of that, to do it like nothing had happened.

Why couldn't he have just gotten all ugly and mean and left me the hell alone? But noooo. He has to be taller, stronger, sexier. And oh God, when I shoved him into the wall of the elevator, I could feel how firm and toned he was underneath. The devil in my mind told me to stop the elevator right there and get some pent-up anger out as he fucked me against the wall.

I can't even stop the blush spreading on my cheeks from thinking about it.

I should hate and despise him for what he did, but I can't get rid of the natural attraction we've always had for each other. And that will never change.

At some point, Jack falls asleep in my lap, like how most of our movie nights go. Once the credits stop rolling, Charlotte lifts the popcorn bowl off of Jack's lap, so I can carry him to bed.

Josh immediately steps in to try to help, but I shake my head. I don't know how many more nights I have left like this with him, so I am definitely not taking a single one for granted. He gets bigger every day.

Soon, he is going to be all independent and not want his mommy carrying him to bed.

Jack's head suddenly moves, but he stays asleep. He just burrows further into my chest. My heart warms, and the backs of my eyes sting.

Nothing in my life compares to this, to my little Jack.

I lay him down in his bed and kiss his forehead. "I love you, little man. Good night."

Studying him for a second longer, I commit every freckle and breath of air to memory before slowly closing the door behind me and heading to my room.

I flop back onto my bed, letting out the heavy sigh that's been sitting in my chest.

I stare up at my ceiling, thoughtless. Scared that if I start thinking about anything, I won't be able to stop.

Sleep is far away, and it won't be visiting me naturally anytime soon. I roll over and grab the bottle off my nightstand—my cure for my restlessness, as a white envelope on my nightstand causes a memory to burst into my mind. The day Alec told me he put the first letter in my mailbox. That letter was just the beginning. Because we wrote each other back and forth every single week after that. We took turns dropping a letter off in each other's mailbox.

We talked about our fears, our hopes, our dreams. Some of our letters were a page long, two pages, or even ten. Just because we wrote to each other constantly, we shared everything in person too. But the letters became tangible things we could hold, read, remember.

I almost wish the letter on my nightstand were from him, and not from a collections agency.

Desperately wanting to push the thoughts of Alec, and of my mom's bill away, I pop two full pills into my mouth and bite the third in half, putting the other half back into the bottle.

I Googled how much melatonin was too much for an adult. And one article said thirty milligrams was dangerous. I stopped reading after that and just convinced myself that as long as I didn't go over that, then I'd be good.

I set the bottle on the nightstand and continue to stare at my ceiling.

Eventually, the melatonin kicks in, finally dragging me under.

Char throws a ridiculously sized bag of chips into the cart, which is definitely not on the list. We continue to meander up and down the aisles until we cross every item off our list—with a few extra things.

We turn to head to the checkout and ram right into someone else's cart.

The words come out automatically. "I'm so sorry. I wasn't watching where I was going."

A familiar deep laugh draws my eyes up. "You're all good. I was hoping to run into you again actually. Although maybe not literally. But this will do." Cam runs his hand along the side of the cart until he's standing right next to me.

Reed is with him, who is about to pounce on Charlotte, oblivious of me being here. He'd better not hurt her. I would hate to leave Jack without a mother while I spent twenty years behind bars.

Cam clears his throat, pulling my attention back to him. "How are you, Laura?"

Well, my ex-boyfriend—the only boyfriend I've ever had—has just temporarily moved back to our hometown. He is pretending like nothing's wrong and hasn't even asked about Jack once. My mom is doing worse. Her vitals have been depleting.

But the truth stays behind my teeth as I respond, "I'm doing fine. What about you?"

He wets his lips. "Just getting ready for this big game coming up. But I'm doing good—better now that I ran into you."

My cheeks can't resist the warmth from his words.

"That's good—a-about the big game, I mean." My words stumble out.

Oh God.

Embarrassment washes over me.

A laugh slips from his lips. "Yeah, are you going?"

"To the game?"

"Well, yeah," he answers immediately, chuckling.

And watch Alec play hockey again? That's a step back in time I don't want to revisit.

"Um, probably not. Sorry, hockey isn't really my thing."

Charlotte scoffs, clearly listening to our conversation. I turn to her and shoot her my mean-mom look.

Hockey is definitely my thing. I just stopped when Alec left. Out of sight, out of mind.

She just shakes her head, laughs, and resumes her conversation with Reed.

Cam isn't stupid. He quickly puts that together. "Well, hopefully, I can convince you to come after all."

Not happening. "Maybe." *Why the fuck did I say that?* There is absolutely no way in hell I will purposely put myself in a room with Alec. "Don't get your hopes up."

Reed whistles Cam over, so they can continue shopping.

But before he turns away, he holds my stare, and it's so intense that I can't look away. "Too late."

Char and I watch them walk off before we get into the checkout lane. The cashier rings us out, and we get the bags loaded into her Camry. She talks the entire time about Reed, barely taking a breath.

When we finally pull out of the parking lot, she takes a break from her nonstop gushing. "So, what do you think about Cam?"

I roll my eyes at her. "Nothing to think about."

She laughs. "Yeah, there are a lot of things to think about. His curly brown hair, his broad shoulders. That gorgeous tan skin. Should I continue?"

I sigh. "I wish you wouldn't."

There is nothing—and will be nothing—going on with Cam. Jack is all I need. If and when I put myself out there again, it definitely won't be with some guy from my ex's hockey team.

Her shoulders slump. "Why don't you just try? You deserve to be happy, Laura. It's about time you get over Alec."

I look over at her, a tightness in my chest at the mention of him. I'm just not ready yet. "I have you, Jack, and Josh. What more could I want?"

"Oh, I don't know … an orgasm?"

"I'll have you know, I am doing just fine by myself. Thank you." I cross my arms.

She laughs again. "Oh yeah, in what department? The getting over Alec or the orgasms?"

I bite back my laugh as we pull into the garage. "Both."

She puts the car in park. "Yeah, well, by yourself doesn't count."

"Oh, yes, it definitely does." I point at her, holding back my laugh.

Over the conversation of my sex life, or lack thereof, I get out of the car and load each arm up as much as I can with groceries.

Josh opens the door right before I get to it. "How are you carrying all of that? It looks like it weighs more than you."

I hastily brush by him, trying to keep the pain from straining my arms off my face. "Maybe I'm just an ant. They can lift, like, five thousand times their weight."

He laughs, heading to help get the rest of the groceries.

Once we get the car unloaded and our haul put away, I slump down onto the couch. Charlotte joins me, laying her head in my lap.

Suddenly, she shoots up and takes off for the kitchen. "Oh my God, I almost forgot!"

She rifles through her purse and pulls out a sheet of paper, hustling back over to the couch.

She thrusts the paper into my hands. "Look! We have to do it. It would totally beat making pizzas for me, and, well, it's a job for you."

Desperately needing any job, I read over the flyer.

Fireflies is now hiring servers. Drop your résumé off to the manager, Mila, digital or paper. On-site interviews.

Working at Fireflies doesn't sound too bad. But honestly, I would probably take any job I can get at the moment. My savings are dwindling away by the second. At this rate, I'll be completely broke in a month.

"You really think we should do it? I haven't been a server before though."

"Psh, who cares? We just have to kill the interview, and we're in." She goes off on a tangent. "Think about it. We would work together, save on gas. We would get to hang out at work and at home, and we'd get to dress up for work in cute outfits and costumes. Give me one con."

Knowing that I don't really have an option, I reply, "Okay, I'm in. When?"

She rips the flyer out of my hands. "It says they are hosting the interviews today and tomorrow from noon to four p.m."

I slap my hands down on my thighs. "Well, I can't tomorrow. I have to go visit Mom at the hospital and take care of some payments. So, we'll have to go today. What time is it?"

She flips her wrist, checking her Apple watch. "One forty-two p.m."

I stand up, already feeling anxious, and pull her up with me. "Okay, let's go get ready."

After an hour of hair and makeup and digging deep in my closet to find the tightest jeans I have, we finally head to Fireflies. I have my résumé on Google Docs on my phone, so I'll just send it to her when we get there.

We pull into the Fireflies parking lot at 2:57 p.m. and head inside. It's so weird to see the place with the lights on. It's a completely different vibe.

There are people running around with decorations and lights—prepping for the night, I assume. One girl runs past with her arms full of blue cutouts shaped like waves. And another has fake seaweed. Under the sea, if I had to guess the theme.

Having no clue what Mila looks like, Charlotte and I just awkwardly stand there, waiting for someone who looks like a Mila.

I nudge Char with my shoulder before whispering to her, "Did the flyer say where to go? Are we just supposed to wait here?"

She doesn't say anything, just shrugs her shoulders. A door opens to the right of us, and three people step out. They shake hands, and two of them go on their way out the door.

One remains—a woman dressed in high-waisted trousers, a tight knit tank top, and stiletto heels.

Talk about intimidating.

She walks over to us, confidence flowing off her in waves. "Are you guys here for the interviews?"

I reach out to shake her outstretched hand. "Yes. Hi, I'm Laura."

She gently shakes my hand and then moves to Charlotte.

She reciprocates. "I'm Charlotte. I'm guessing you're Mila."

She casually tucks her hands into her trouser pockets. "That's me." She turns, continuing to talk to us, "Do you guys have a résumé with you? If not, don't worry; it's not a problem. Right this way."

We scuttle after her, trying to keep up with her stride. This woman is a power walker.

We step through the doorway to an office. It has a large desk in the center with papers stacked every which way. She takes her seat behind the desk and gestures to the two chairs in front of it.

She rapidly types stuff out on her phone before stowing it away in her desk drawer. "Let's get started. Why don't you guys tell me a little bit about yourselves?" She gestures her hand out to me to start.

I clear my throat before my professional voice instinctively kicks in. "It's great to meet you. My name is Laura. I'm twenty-two years old. I grew up here and have been to Fireflies a couple of times. It seems like such a fun place to work." I look to Charlotte to show that I have ended my introduction.

She takes the cue and settles into the chair, crossing her legs. Her bubbly voice is ready to shine. "I'm Charlotte. I'm twenty-two. I grew up here as well—with Laura in fact." She flashes her award-winning smile at me. "We were here last weekend when you guys had the fae theme. It was so fun, and the energy was insane. We would love to be a part of this."

My attention returns to Mila. She continues to ask us a few questions about our previous work. She also asks us more about ourselves. I like that she seems like she genuinely wants to get to know us instead of it being some dumb interview where you don't even crack the surface.

After what feels more like having lunch than sitting in an interview, she says, "All right, ladies, well, I think you both would be an incredible fit for the team. You're young and fun, you seem quick-witted, and you'll be a catch with our crowds."

After going over paperwork, pay, and expectations, Mila offers her hand to each of us to shake. She gives us a sheet of paper with the next five dress-up themes, which we'll need to get costumes for. She doesn't like doing matching ones because she wants everyone to feel comfortable and be able to show their own style.

I know I haven't even started yet, but so far, so good. And now, Char and I have a shopping trip in the near future, which is something I'm actually looking forward to. Hopefully, we'll find some good sales.

Our first shift is this upcoming Saturday. The club doesn't open until nine, but we have to be here at seven to go over some training and help prep.

When the door of the club closes behind us, we finally celebrate, and Char aggressively pulls me into a hug.

"Oh my God, we did it!" I squeal to her.

She thrashes me around with her continuous happy dance. "Let's go celebrate at home!" She turns on her heels and takes off for the car, not looking back.

I laugh to myself and chase after her.

Fireflies annoyingly reminds me of Alec.

He will be leaving soon enough anyway, so I just need to push him to the back of my mind and keep him there. Out of sight, out of mind.

If only it were that easy.

I shift the car in park before leaning my head against the steering wheel. Closing my eyes, I take a deep breath. I normally come on Sundays, but since tonight is my first shift at Fireflies, I want tomorrow to just hang out and recover from the late night that I'm sure it will be.

I left Jack at home this time. I don't want him to see her in the shape she's in. The doctor called earlier this week and said that her vitals have been deteriorating. They don't know how to fix her.

When she had her stroke, her heart stopped for a few minutes, which meant that her brain wasn't getting any oxygen. They have done everything they can. It's up to her to come back to us. Right now, we just wait.

I don't register anything on the walk to her room. I think I take the elevator, but I don't remember pressing any buttons.

Seeing her like this is unbearable. I can't *not* visit because no matter how bad she gets, this could be my last time seeing her. Every time could be the last time. This pain is insufferable, but one day, I will wish I could feel it just one more time. Because she will be gone … for good.

I don't know how I'm going to even process that, let alone tell Jack. He idolizes her. But it's weird; sometimes, I feel like kids are better at dealing with death than adults. Maybe it's a time thing—because we've known them longer. Or maybe kids are just purer, less selfish. They want their loved ones to have peace, be pain-free.

But me? I'm definitely selfish.

I turn the handle on her door, and my heart constricts. Her cheekbones have sunken in more. Her skin is paler than normal.

She looks … well, she looks like death.

My feet find their way to my chair, and I scoot up next to her, taking her hand in mine. A lump instantly grows in my throat. I open my mouth to speak, but nothing comes out.

I drop my head down to our intertwined hands.

Mom … come on. Mom, just wake up. Please. I can't speak the words out loud. That would make this far too real.

I just want her to hug me, to hold me, to tell me everything will be okay. I just want her back.

The lump grows but refuses to burst free. I want to cry. I want to let everything out—every ounce of pain, frustration, anguish. But nothing comes. The dam is just too well built.

Stroking my thumb over her cool hand, I start singing the lullaby she used to sing to me every night as a kid. "*Lullaby and good night, with roses bedight. With lilies o'er spread is baby's wee bed.*" Each word gets quieter and quieter as I go, drifting into silence again.

"I love you, Mom. Come back to me." My lips press into the bluish skin on her hand.

I spend a good hour or two just sitting with her. I tell her about the job and the fun costumes and stuff. She would be excited for me but maybe a little hesitant that it's at a nightclub.

I avoid the Alec topic at all costs, but he keeps popping his way into my mind.

I don't speak of him once, but I definitely think of him repeatedly. And his stupid smile.

I feel a little better after leaving the hospital, having vented to my mom and getting out some of my frustrations.

Charlotte and I have to go shopping today.

Every Saturday, there's a theme. Something fun, sometimes a little crazy. Tonight's theme is angels—dark or light, up to us. I think Char wants to get a dark angel costume, but I'll probably just stick to the classic white-winged angel.

But we have absolutely nothing to put toward this look—or any of the other looks for that matter. Next weekend is vampires, then it's witches, then mermaids, then pirates, and then God knows what.

It does have a magical quality to it. Like stepping out of reality, which can be nice. Especially right now.

When I pull up to the house, Jack is outside, playing catch with Josh. Thankfully, Josh's school is only part-time right now. So, he is always the one to pick Jack up and drop him off whenever I can't.

Honestly, I'd be lost without him and Char. Hands down, I would not be able to do this alone.

Jack misses the catch when I draw his attention. He immediately lights up, waving to me. I can't help the smile that stretches across my face.

Pulling into the garage, I barely get my door a foot open before Jack is trying to get in the car and onto my lap.

Laughs burst out of me. "Hi, buddy. How was your day?"

He throws his arms around my neck, pulling me into a tight hug, and my heart sinks to the floor. "I missed you, Mom."

Sometimes, it's too much—the love I have for this little human that I made.

I wrap my arms around his small body. "I missed you too."

We sit in our hug for a moment before the little ball of energy needs to move again. I swear he has Red Bull pumping through his veins.

He hops off my lap and takes off for the yard again.

My brain hasn't fully caught up with the present. It's still in that hospital bed, stuck in that stale room.

I grab my bag and drag myself inside. I'm in no mood to go shopping. I'll have to make something work for this costume from my own closet.

Would I be the world's worst employee if I called in sick on the first day?

Ugh.

I glide up the stairs to my room, wishing I could've stayed with my mom longer—or not gone at all. I can't get the image of her out of my head; it's burned in place.

I kick my door open, and my jaw falls to the floor. My eyes burn. Sprawled on the bed are fluffy white angel wings; a gold halo headband; a low-cut, long-sleeved white bodysuit; and a white faux leather miniskirt.

Next to it are about ten shopping bags stuffed full of what I can tell are all the costumes I could ever need.

"You didn't answer my text. And when you're with her, that normally means it's bad. So, I thought I'd do this part for you." Charlotte comes up behind me, wrapping her arms around my shoulders.

I can't find the words. I can't find anything. I'm utterly frozen, completely overwhelmed.

She just squeezes me harder, kissing the side of my head. "I love you, Lu. I'm always here if you need to talk."

Lifting my hands up, I squeeze her arms. My voice is hoarse, quieter than a pin dropping. "I love you too, Char." My eyes fall shut as I revel in the contact given by my best friend.

After what feels like seconds or maybe hours, she pulls away, leaving me with my heavy thoughts.

I make my way to my bed, in shock with the haul. She really went all out. Grabbing the closest bag, I dump it onto my bed.

Red devil horns fall out along with a lacy bodysuit, which, holy moly, should probably never be worn in public. But I mean, I'd get hundred-dollar tips in this outfit. Although they might think it's a different kind of club.

I move to the next bag, finding glue-on fangs, red eye contacts, and an exposing outfit to go with it.

After emptying out all the contents of the haul, I stare at it in awe. She got everything I could possibly need. And the girl knows my sizes.

I put everything away, except for the angel costume. I roll the tote out from under my bed, which stores my less-worn shoes. I know I have a gold pair of heels or something in here somewhere.

I lift up my black thigh-highs, and *ta-da*, I reach in, pulling out the chunky gold heels. They're absolutely stunning. I've only ever worn them once, but I'm glad I held on to them because they're perfect for this. The thick heels are all bejeweled. And they lace up my calf about three inches above the heel counter.

Oh, I'm going to feel incredible in this.

After curling every strand of my brown hair, I head downstairs and take over for Josh. After a couple more hours of trying to tire Jack out, it's crunch time.

I walk into my bathroom with a little pep in my step. I think this job could really be something great in my life right now. It is definitely pushing me out of my comfort zone wardrobe wise.

Reaching into my makeup bag, I pull out my foundation and begin applying it with my sponge, noticing the little smile on my lips.

Once my makeup is done and I have highlighted the shit out of my face and applied a clear gloss, I change into my outfit for the night. I normally would have changed into my outfit before putting my makeup on because putting a top on after makeup, especially a white top, is fucking hard. But thankfully, I'm wearing a bodysuit tonight.

I step into my new long-sleeved bodysuit and slip my white leather skirt on. Finishing the look off with my heels.

To be honest, I could get used to these dress-up nights. I haven't had this much confidence in years.

Grabbing my angel wings and my purse, I head downstairs to Char, who's been waiting on me for a solid twenty minutes.

She expels the most dramatic sigh when I finally step into the living room. "About damn time." She turns to me. Her eyes bulging. "Hot damn, Mama! Look at you!"

I give her a little twirl while laughing. "Not so bad yourself!"

Her dark angel costume is killer, almost an exact opposite look of mine. She has a long-sleeved black bodysuit on with a black leather skirt and heels, a black halo, and wings—of course.

"Hey, guys. Have a good ni—" Josh cuts off when he sees us. His lips tip into a half-smile. "Well, I think I might just be able to quit my job. Because you guys are going to make us rich tonight."

I purse my lips, suppressing the chuckle wanting to escape. "No, sir, you definitely cannot. Not with how much Charlotte spent on these outfits. Plus, you do data entry from home. Like, shut up. It's the easiest job ever, and you're making bank."

He walks up to us and gives each of us a kiss on the cheek. "You both look great. Have a good night. Be safe. Call if you need me."

Char and I both lean in to give him a kiss on the cheek at the same time, leaving nice, sticky lip prints on his cheeks.

"Bye, Joshie." Char wiggles her fingers at him as we head out the door.

After we get in the car and Char starts the engine, music blasts through her speakers, deafening me. I've never smacked a button so hard in my life.

"Oh my God, do you really have to listen to your music that loud?" I laugh and am partially in shock that she has any hearing left at all.

She gives me her famous side-eye and snickers. "Yes, actually, I do. It's a full-body experience."

I can't resist my laugh at her. "Luckily, you'll only get about another five years before you can't listen to anything."

"Ha-ha." She mocks.

We drive the short distance to Fireflies with the music at a low volume—thank goodness. I try to calm my nerves as much as I can, but the closer we get, the worse it becomes, and the tighter this skirt feels.

When we finally pull into the employee parking lot, I am ready to jump out of my skin.

I'm not usually nervous for a new job, but I really don't want to mess this up. I need this money, and I'm not going to find another job that pays this well for a college student.

I let Char lead the way through the back entrance, and an oversize bodybuilder opens the door for us.

The man leads us to the employee lounge to drop our stuff off before heading to the main room.

When he pushes the door open with an *Employees Only* sign, my steps falter.

An employee lounge? Ha! This feels like it should be the VIP lounge for the most pristine guests.

A giant glass chandelier hangs from the center of the raised ceiling. Lounge chairs line the wall with small round tables accompanying each one.

"Are you kidding me right now? You're seeing this too, right?" Char walks ahead of me into the room and heads toward the door labeled *Lockers*.

I trail quickly behind her, still in shock.

The wall of lockers doesn't disappoint either. Although we quickly drop the shocked act because there are two other girls in here. They are talking in a hushed tone but end their convo when we get closer.

Their costumes look great.

One of them has a cute blonde pixie cut, and she's decked out with white glitter for the night. She's literally shimmering under the lights. I can't wait to see it under the flashing lights in the main room. She offers a sweet smile when she turns our way.

The brunette grins as she turns to us, and she is the first one to speak. "First day? Laura and Charlotte, right?"

I'm stunned at the fact that they already know our names and still a little shook with the decor, so my response is lagging. "Yeah, I'm Laura, and this is Charlotte."

They each introduce themselves and offer their hands, and we shake them. The brunette's name is Hannah, and she is a shift lead. The pixie blonde girl's name is Callie, and she is a bartender. And also Hannah's best friend.

They show us where to clock in and out on the computer system back here.

After we briefly talk to them, we follow them through the door of the locker room that leads to the main corridor of the building. Music is pouring out of the main room—aka the club. The DJ must be setting up.

Hannah and Callie follow the music and take us with them. It seems so much bigger with all the lights on. The DJ is set up on the stage on top of the bar. I really do work at the coolest place.

The circle bar's entrance and exit is a small break in the bar top that you can just go through. Mila is talking to two guys when we approach. They look like bartenders based on their aprons.

The music is intense inside the bar with the DJ up above us. My listening skills will need to be on point. Good thing I've raised a toddler, so I am fluent in gibberish. Drunk people and babies speak the same language.

We grab Mila's attention as we approach. She isn't dressed up in a costume like the rest of us. She's rocking leggings, a black bralette, and an open blazer.

"Nice to see you two. Your costumes look great. This is Mark and Eli, two of my best bartenders. They have each been here over a year. They are going to get your training started. I hope you're quick learners. Lights off in ten." And with that, she walks off and out of the room.

Char offers her hand to the boys, who each take it. "I'm Charlotte, and this is Laura."

After shaking Charlotte's hand, they shake mine, and I catch Eli's gaze drifting a little too low. Yeah, one more time, and I'll put him in his place.

I know my boobs are practically on show in this top right now. I expect the ogling from drunk customers. But I expect respect from my coworkers.

Mark grabs a binder from below the bar and flips it open. "Tonight, you guys will mostly be handing out drinks and running them to tables. Your mixing training isn't till the next shift. That takes a little more time to get the hand of. But this binder is here when you need a quick reference if you can't remember a drink. You'll pick it up as you go from watching us to making your own." He slides the binder back under the bar top. "We'll get into that more next time."

Char and I are intently watching him, trying to take in as much as we can. He shifts a couple of feet over to one of the computer screens.

"Here, I'm going to show you how to enter a tab and how to ring a customer out. You guys will help us out with that tonight while we mix the drinks; it'll cut the time down between customers."

We get up behind him and watch him tap through a bunch of buttons. It seems pretty simple; it basically walks you through it. The first option on the screen is *single* or *tab*. If you click *single*, it just pulls up the screen to enter the drink and bill the card. If you select *tab*, it will pull up all the already-open ones and has an option for adding one.

After we finish going through some quick computer training, he shows us how all of the tables are set up and how to figure out which drink goes where.

Near the walls of the room are round tables. Each table has a built-in mini ordering tablet—locked into the table, of course. Anyone who orders from them has to have a tab set up, so we don't have to worry about handling any of the money. Each table is numbered with a light on the wall above it. I can't believe I've never noticed them before.

Eli explains that they split the bar into a semicircle—two bartenders taking one half and two on the other.

He takes us through a mock order, and I'd like to say we are doing pretty damn good. After a couple more tips and tricks from the boys, Callie and Hannah join back up with us after doing some prep work on their half of the bar.

"How do you guys feel? You ready?" Callie asks, hopping up onto the counter.

Char answers for us, immediately going into conversation with all of them. It's always been so easy for her like that.

I like the group though; it seems like we'll all get along. And everyone seems nice so far, so that's a plus. My gaze and mind shift back to the table numbers on the wall. I'm in disbelief that I didn't notice them.

"… ass grab," Hannah says, immediately grabbing my attention.

"Wait, what?" I ask.

"I was saying that if any guys—or girls for that matter—get a little too handsy tonight, let Claude or Axel know. They will get them out in no time. Honestly, they will probably be the one pulling them off you. They're really good about keeping us safe." Hannah pulls Callie off the counter as Mila approaches.

"Good to know. Thanks," I tell her.

"No problem. We take care of each other here. If someone is making you uncomfortable, let us know. Mila doesn't put up with that bullshit," Callie adds in.

Mila leans back against the counter. "Damn straight. Five minutes out. Lights off in two."

Someone near the door grabs her attention.

"Duty calls." She pushes off the counter.

The last few prep minutes are spent laughing and joking around with the group, and before we know it, the lights go off, and the floor beneath my feet lights up.

With no one walking on it, except Axel and Claude, it reacts to the music.

Dear God, how much money does this place make?

The music above us is thumping, and if I thought that was loud, I stand corrected. Because the second those doors open, it sounds like thunder is booming through the room. I had no idea people could make such noise.

The first couple transactions are slow, but Char and I soon catch on, and after an hour in, we are killing it. It feels like I've been doing this forever. It is so easy to settle into.

"Laura!" Mark shouts to me over the music.

I take off for him, ready to input and process the order.

But when I approach, curly brown hair and blue eyes I recognize are looking back at me. His eyes drop quickly, taking in my body, and I feel my blush follow his stare.

Cam has a way of making me feel his gaze. But if Cam is here, that can only mean one thing—Alec is here somewhere too.

"I like the costume." Cam winks at me. "Can I steal you for a dance later?"

Mark steps slightly in front of me, turning his face to me. "Do you know him? I can send him out if you don't."

I rest a reassuring hand on his shoulder and nod my head. "Yeah, I know him. He's a friend."

"All right." He grabs Cam's card and goes to input it himself.

"Protective, is he?" Cam's lip twitches as he nods to Mark, tracking him with his eyes.

"We all are of each other. We don't put up with the *creeps*." I smirk at him.

"So, now, I'm a creep?" He stretches his hand closer to mine. "How about that dance?"

I get flashbacks of the last time we danced together. *Whew, I think it just got warmer in here.* The flashback shifts, and I imagine Alec behind me with his strong hands on my hips. *Fuck.*

There's no way I can dance with Cam, knowing Alec's here somewhere. I don't want anything from Alec, but I can guarantee that I would be seeing more of him if I let Cam grind and feel me up like he did last time.

"Maybe next time. It's my first night. I'm trying to make a good impression." I shrug my shoulders, trying to play it off.

"Is this about Kos?" he asks me blatantly.

I immediately shake my head—maybe a little too hard. "No. What? Why would you say that?" My words lack the confidence they need.

"I see the way he looks at you, even in the few brief instances it's been, and I know you guys have a history."

Mark returns and slides him his card.

"I'll catch you later, Laura." Cam smiles and shakes his head, walking off.

History? What did Alec say about us? He looks at me? A thousand questions flood my mind, and I'd be lying if I said that butterflies weren't flying around in my stomach right now.

Eli calls me over, and off again I go. He has a tray of drinks ready to go to a table. "Number eight. Thanks, Laura." He turns and greets the next customer.

I load the tray in my arms and carefully make my way to table eight, making sure I am constantly aware of the dancers and tipsy people all around me.

The table is full of guys, all a bit older than me. Maybe late twenties, older thirties.

"Hello, boys," I greet them flirtatiously. I want the tips as big as I can make them.

The one on the right leans back in his chair and slowly scans me head to toe, but a cold shiver follows his gaze.

Tips, tips, tips.

I pass out the drinks and set the last on a coaster next to an empty stool.

Making my way back to the front of the table, I fold the tray across my chest. "Can I get you boys anything else?"

A tingling sensation burns into the side of my head, and I turn to the table a few down.

My stomach drops to the floor.

Some prissy blonde is practically trying to put her boobs in Alec's face, but when I look at him, his gaze is locked on to me. My whole body heats up, and I quickly turn back to my table.

Each of them is looking at some part of me, but none of them are meeting my eyes. I clearly have all of their attention.

The one on the right leans forward, a little too close to my face. "How about your number?" He reaches out and tries to touch my cheek.

I start to take a step back, but big arms go around my waist, and a wave of alcohol floods my nose. Looking up, I see the occupant of the empty stool. He pulls me tighter against him, and every hair on my body is standing up. I want to scream, but nothing comes out.

All of a sudden, I'm ripped out of his grasp and pulled into another set of strong arms. But these are firmer yet gentler. They hold me like I'm important, like I matter, like I'm theirs.

Hearing a grunt, I turn and see Cam punch the handsy guy straight in the nose, and a popping sound rings in my ears. But if Cam's fighting him, then who's—

"Are you all right, Lu?" Alec's voice warms my ear and neck.

He spins me in his arms and looks me over for visible injuries. I can't help the giggle that comes out of me. A big smile instantly breaks across his lips, creasing the dimple in his left cheek.

"What's so funny?" He lightly shakes his head.

"He was feeling me up; you won't find any cuts or bruises." I'm still giggling and starting to think that maybe I'm not so okay after all.

His gaze shoots to the guy behind me, still being held up by Cam and the rest of the team.

If looks could kill.

When his gaze returns to me, all the harshness is gone. "Are you okay?" His fingers start slowly rubbing up and down my arms where he's holding me.

My breathing slows, and I can feel my heart gradually calm down.

I nod my head. "Yeah, th-thank you."

He pulls me closer to him, and I let him. His fingers continue to soothe me, keeping a consistent rhythm. And maybe it's the adrenaline talking—definitely the adrenaline talking—but I wish he would use his fingers and that rhythm on a certain spot between my legs.

Nope. That's wrong! Stop thinking about his hand between your legs. Dammit.

When he rests his chin on my head, I inhale a sharp breath, and a whole different feeling washes over me. It's like being back in time. Except now, he's built like Hercules, and he could bench, like, two of me. Alec holding me like this makes the world around us disappear.

But I can't find comfort in this. I just can't.

I pull out of his arms. "I have to get back to work. Thanks again."

Turning to see if the missing boy is still alive, I find no one there. The missing guy and his buddies are long gone, probably thanks to Axel or Claude—or both. Cam and the team are gone too.

Alec grabs my wrist, but his touch is as light as a feather. "Lu, wait."

I turn, giving him back my attention even though my mind is telling me not to.

He rubs the back of his neck, rocking his weight back and forth, still lightly holding my wrist. "Can I see you sometime? Coffee, lunch, dinner, whatever you want."

My chest warms at his question. But I can't deny the fact that the only reason we aren't together right now is because of him.

But with my mom being sick, I've learned one thing. Life is short, and most of the time, it fucking sucks. So, when something makes you happy or even brings you an ounce of joy, you grab on to it, and you never let go.

Fuck, I'm going to regret this.

"Yes."

When we get home, I crawl under my covers, eager to fall asleep. But seconds of tossing and turning build to minutes and then an hour.

Why am I so restless?

My mind automatically starts replaying tonight's events like a movie. When it gets to the part where Alec's rough hands were on me, I start to get an idea of why I can't sleep.

My hand drifts under the covers, finding the waistband of my panties. My eyelids flutter closed as I imagine Alec's hands on me again, on them trailing down my arms, onto my sides, sliding between my legs—

STOP.

Fucking hell.

I switch the main character out in my mind to someone with no strings attached.

Brown curls and bright blue eyes come into view.

Cam and I are alone in my room.

I face the wall as I slip my shirt, bra, pants, and panties off.

"I've wanted to do this since I saw you," Cam growls as he races toward me.

The cool wall against my face does nothing to lessen the fire burning between my legs. He wraps one of his large hands around both of mine, locking them behind my back. He slides his foot between mine, and in one motion, he widens my stance.

Cam leans into me. Pressing his nose into my hair, he inhales deeply. His voice is raspy and deep. "Laura."

A shiver rolls down my back, causing me to push backward into him.

He moans and bites down on my earlobe. "So. Fucking. Sexy." With each word, he sucks on my ear.

Cam releases my wrists and spins me around to face him.

I'm panting. My fingers pick up pace as my legs fall open wider.

Cam boxes me in with his arms. His gaze is carnivorous, and he is about to devour me.

He drops to his knees and looks up into my hooded eyes. "Watch me."

My tongue wets my lips as he trails his hand from my ankle, up to the slight bend of my knee, to the highest point of my inner thigh. He repeats the motion with his other hand.

Placing a hand on either side of my entrance, he studies my sex, memorizing every crease and fold before glancing up once more and saying with pure desire, "So. Fucking. Sexy."

He gasps and his tongue laps against me. He seals his lips over me, sucking with ferocity, and then his tongue flicks over and over.

Biting down on my lip, I circle harder, faster, feeling release nearing.

My fingers thread in Cam's hair, pushing him against me. He slides a finger into me, pumping in and out. A second joins, and my toes curl into the floor.

So close.
I circle faster and faster, but release won't come.
Harder and harder.

Cam stands up and drops his pants and boxers in one motion. He hooks one arm under my leg and pulls me toward him. His huge cock throbs against my thigh.

He lines himself up with my wet entrance and thrusts hard and fast inside me. I yelp in pain and pleasure. He doesn't wait for me to adjust. He thrusts into me again, and I cry out his name.

Frustration creeps into my mind. I should've come already. *Fuck!*

Cam fucks me harder and harder, faster and faster.

My body craves more, needs more. But Cam can't give it to me.

Fine! FINE!

A strong, callous hand wraps around my throat. My jaw unhinges with desire.

"Be a good girl for me, Lu," Alec's husky voice sings in my ear. "Watch me make you come."

My eyes unevenly flutter open, and darkened hazel eyes pierce my core.

Alec pulls out until his tip starts to slip out of me. He slams back into me hard, picking up the pace with every thrust.

His grip on my throat tightens, and he lifts my leg higher, hitting deeper inside of me.

"Come on, Lu," Alec demands. "You're taking it so well. Good girl," he praises.

I bite down on my lip as I fall headfirst, spiraling into bliss.

Fucking Alec. Stupid, stupid Alec.

Laura,

I am writing you this letter because I'm scared I won't be able to say all of this in person.

Since we met, everything in my life has gotten better. School, skating, hockey.

I know that we haven't been together long, but I'm falling so hard for you, Lu. You make me smile every day. You are my first thought in the morning, and my last before I fall asleep.

I know what we have is special, one of a kind.

When you walk into a room, I feel your presence before I see you. In the hallways, I find you in the sea of our classmates.

People will say that we are crazy for being so attached. But we are meant for each other, Lu. We are just the lucky ones that happen to find each other so young.

I would do anything for you, I want you to have the world, the universe, all the planets, moons, and stars. I want to make you the happiest girl in the world. And I will. I always will.

Because I love you so much, Laura.

When I see you again, I'm going to tell you in person how much I love you, I'm going to scream it to the world for all to hear.

It would mean the world to hear you say it back, but please don't feel any pressure until you're ready.

That's why I wrote it in this letter, so that you would feel comfortable to say it when you want, not because I said it and you feel obligated in the moment.

I hope you have the most amazing dreams tonight, hopefully I'm staring in them. ;)

Love, Alec

"Class dismissed. Laura, please hang back a second," Mrs. Lang announces to the room.

Everyone immediately packs their things while trying to look around to see who Laura is. I give them a minute to get going before I head down the steps to her desk.

"What can I do for you?" I ask her politely.

She leans comfortably back in her chair. "You are doing exceptionally well in my class."

I flush at her compliment. I work my ass off for my grades. "Thank you."

She sits forward, crossing her hands on her desk. "I'm quite involved in the community, and I have an opportunity I think you might be interested in."

I'm definitely intrigued. "Okay, what is it?"

"An acquaintance of mine at The Crooked Spine wants to hire someone local for some marketing work. He gave me the task of finding someone for it. They need someone to design a marketing plan for this next year. It would be a paid temporary position, and you could work remotely from home. It would only require about eight hours a week from you at the most. Do you think you'd be interested?"

I think my jaw is on the floor by the time she's done. The Crooked Spine is a bookstore company that spans the US. But our location just opened up. I attended their opening just last month. It would be amazing for my résumé. And it would just be plain fun, and it's exactly what I want to do after school.

I nod my head as I finally get ahold of my tongue. "Yes. That would be amazing. Thank you so much for thinking of me."

She smiles at me. "Of course. I will have him email you." She quickly jots down the contact info and hands me the sticky note. "Have a good weekend, Laura."

I take the slip from her, unable to contain the grin on my face. "Thank you so much."

Once I leave the room, I fumble to get my phone out of my pocket as fast as I can. I want to tell Char right away even though I'll see her in minutes because she's picking me up.

She answers on the first ring. "Sup, babe?"

"Guess what just happened!" The words practically squeak out of me.

"What? *Out of the way, asshole*!" she shouts way too loud into the phone. "Sorry about that. I swear this person is doing, like, five miles an hour."

I can't help but laugh at her. "Dear God, Char, you have more road rage than Josh, and that's saying something."

"Ugh, whatever." I can practically see her roll her eyes. "What happened? Wait, let me guess. You ran into Cam, and you guys went at it in the elevator."

"Funny. No. My professor recommended me for a marketing job for The Crooked Spine. It's super-duper part-time, but it pays, and, like, it's actually what I'm going to school for, ya know?" I bite my lip, just trying to bathe in the moment.

"Lu, that's amazing! I'm so proud of you." I hear her blinker click on in her car. "I'm here, north door."

I add a little bit more juice in my step and head out of the building. "Coming." I end the call.

I hop in the car, and—oh my gosh—we weren't even off the phone for more than a minute, and her music is already blaring. I immediately turn it down.

"You're no fun, Mom." She mocks, pulling out of the lot.

Smacking her hard on the shoulder, I laugh. "Shut up, you brat. You ready for tonight?"

"Hell yes, I am. I've been waiting all day to get ready. Callie and Hannah are going to love our costumes tonight; we'll be the cutest vampires around." Excitement is oozing off of her.

"Thanks to you." If she hadn't been amazing and done all the shopping, I'd probs be stuck, wearing whatever I could pull from the back of my closet.

"It's what I'm here for." She blows me an air kiss.

We talk the rest of the way home about how we should do our hair. She also fills me in on her and Reed. They went on a date last night, and apparently, he is quite the romancer.

I'm happy for her. She deserves nothing but the best.

We pull into the driveway seconds before Josh and Jack pull in behind us. Josh picks him up from school because his schedule is open. I buy him extra ice cream and snacks to make up for it.

But I know he really does it for Jack. Uncle Josh loves that boy as much as I do.

Jack slams his door and takes off for me. "Mom!"

He barrels into me, and I feel nothing but absolute love for my boy.

"Hey, little man. How was school?"

He wraps his hand around mine and leads me inside, telling me all about kindergarten. "Today, we went over more spelling stuff; it wasn't very fun. But Erick was helping me a lot."

Erick is Jack's best friend. He just spent the night last weekend, and I swear the boys didn't get a minute of sleep.

"I can help you, too, if you want. I'm pretty good at spelling." I squeeze his warm hand.

"Yeah, okay." He shrugs and bolts up the stairs to his room.

I lean backward over the couch and fall back against the cushions, landing with a soft thud. I close my eyes and revel in the one moment of calm I will have today.

I scoot fully onto the couch and tuck one of the pillows under my head. Before I know it, one minute turns to five, which turns to ten and then turns to sleep.

My shoulder is shaking, but I don't want to get up yet. My shoulder moves again.

"Get up, or I'm dragging you off this couch."

Since when did my subconscious sound like Charlotte?

My shoulders move again, and then I'm flying. And when I land, it hurts, and reality floods my vision.

"Oww." My voice is all sleepy.

Charlotte is standing over me in her robe with her hair wrapped in a towel. "I warned you." She shrugs and heads to the stairs. "You've got an hour."

Ugh, work.

Don't get me wrong; I really like Fireflies, but I could've stayed in that nap forever. I haven't napped that deeply in a long time.

I drag my sleepy self upstairs and head to my room to start getting ready.

I grab the tight leather leggings and long-sleeved black crop top. Digging through my new box of props and random stuff for costumes, I pull out the red contacts and knee-high black boots.

After spending the next forty-five minutes curling my hair and doing my makeup, I squeeze myself into the leather leggings, scared I might never be able to get them off.

I finish my look with a red lip to match the red contacts. Honestly, I look hot.

I adjust my top tighter to keep the girls a little more secure, but boy, are they popping in this shirt. Let's see if I can pull four hundred in tips tonight.

I really don't know how we both got lucky enough to get a job at this club. It's the hottest one in town, and everyone applies there. And people rarely leave because the money is insane, especially on the weekends.

I meet Charlotte downstairs in the kitchen. While she talks with Josh, I turn to see Jack watching some cartoons in the living room. My big flannel jacket covers me all up while I walk up to Jack and give him a big kiss on the forehead, red lipstick and all.

He writhes away. "Ugh, Mom! There's stuff on your lips!"

He cringes and tries to wipe it off, but I can't help but giggle. I lick my thumb and quickly get it off his face before it sets.

"Be good for Josh. I love you." I blow him a kiss, and he leans up and fake catches it.

"You love me, even in the rain?" he asks me, our habitual routine rolling off his tongue.

"Even in the storm." I smile.

With that, he turns his attention back to the cartoons.

I remember the day we started that. It was after Mom went into a coma, and Jack went with me to visit her for the first time. It was pouring rain, and the sky was a thousand hues of gray.

He's scared of lightning, like most kids. And when I told him that Grandma and I loved him, no matter what, he asked me if I'd still love him, even when it rained, even when it was scary. I thought it was silly at the time, but now, it's just become our little routine. And I wouldn't change a thing about it.

When we get to Fireflies, Char and I head in the employee door, clock in, and put all of our stuff away. The last few shifts we had were all about mixing drinks and memorizing the menu. We are mostly still serving and billing tonight, but we get to help make some drinks for the first time.

We meet up with the rest of the crew at the bar to help finish setting up, and before we know it, the lights are off, and people are pouring in.

By the end of the night, I have a little over four hundred and fifty dollars in my apron and the biggest smile on my face. No creeps tonight, which was great. And we pulled in huge tips. Everyone made out really well.

Char and I are the last to leave, so we offer to finish wiping down. When we are finally leaving, it's a little past three a.m. Claude walks us to her car, leading the way.

He stops abruptly, causing me to crash into his back, which feels an awful lot like a brick wall.

I step out around him, but he puts his arm out to stop me from going forward.

"Who are you?" His voice booms out to someone ahead of us.

I finally manage to get around the telephone pole–sized arm of his. And when I do, I can't help the flutters setting ablaze in my stomach and chest.

"It's okay, Claude. I know him," I reassure him before he walks off.

Char giggles behind me.

Leaning against his motorcycle is Alec himself. He is grinning ear to ear when I finally meet his gaze.

I walk up to him with a thousand questions on the tip of my tongue, but not a word will come out. I'm scared once I start, I won't stop.

He sets the helmet he's holding on the seat before taking a step toward me. "Sorry to just show up. Reed said you guys were working tonight. And I wanted to see you. So, I thought I'd offer you a ride home. If you want it, of course."

He smiles, and his gaze drops to my open jacket. He wets his bottom lip. "You're gorgeous, Lu. I mean, you always were, but now … whew, absolutely beautiful." He holds my stare the whole time.

I want to say, *Find another girl to break*.

Spinning on my heels, I have every intention to run off. But my body has something else in mind. It ignites from his words, and I can still feel the caress from his eyes. I spin back around to face him, wanting to smack myself.

Words are still struggling to come out. It's really annoying how easy they seem to be for him. "Um, thank you."

My eyes fall to his open leather bomber jacket. He's wearing a plain white T-shirt underneath it. But boy, I didn't know that could look so good. I can see how he fills it out, and I can't imagine what he looks like without it.

Ever been disgusted with yourself?

He clears his throat. It's hard to believe this is the same boy I loved so many years ago.

"How about that ride?" He smirks.

One thing hasn't changed. That smirk of his still melts me to the core. *Dammit.* But this is all we'll ever be—short sentences and longing.

I turn to see if Charlotte is waiting in her car. But when I look, there are no other cars in the lot.

Oh my God, that little bitch left me. Oh, she's going to hear about this later.

Well, it looks like I'm walking.

I pull my coat around my waist. "Look, Alec, I agreed to catch up, and I am still willing to. But not tonight. Thanks for the offer, but I'm okay. I'm just gonna walk; it's only a few blocks." *More like ten.* I on my heel and start heading home.

He brings the bike to life, and I hear him catching up to me.

"Laura, you can't be serious. There is no way in hell I'm letting you walk home. Especially alone in that damn outfit."

What did he just say?

I slam my foot on the ground and abruptly turn around, and stomp up to him where he has stopped the bike. "Excuse me?" I shove my finger in his face. "One, you have no right when it comes to my choices. Two, if I want to walk home, I will. Because that is my decision. And three, keep your opinion of my outfit to yourself."

I take off again, trying to leave him behind. The engine growls.

Fuck.

"Laura, come on. That's not what I meant. I'm sorry. Just let me take you home. Please," he pleads with me.

I remain silent, continuing my strut home.

"Laura, come on." He keeps pace with me. "I just want you to get home safe, that's all. I couldn't live with myself if something happened because I rode off."

"I can get home by myself, Alec, I've been doing it for quite a while. Thank you." I stumble a step. If it wasn't for this pent-up, boiling anger inside me, I would give in to the throbbing pain in my feet right now.

"Whatever, Lu. Get on the bike; don't get on the bike. I'm still going to be here the whole way back to your house." I can hear the annoyance growing in his voice.

But I don't care right now.

We walk the next thirty or so feet in silence when the first drop hits my cheek.

You've got to be kidding me.

I keep walking, pretending I didn't feel it. But I can only do that for about another five more feet before the heavens split open and rain begins pouring down on us.

When the first strike of lightning hits, I jump a little.

He rides ahead of me, parks the bike, and hops up onto the sidewalk, blocking my path. "If you don't get on this damn bike right now, I'll put you there myself." He stalks up to me with the helmet in his hand. "I'm wet, annoyed, and pissed the fuck off that you won't just let me help you. I just want to get you home safe—that's it. Stop making this so hard." He drops the helmet in the grass and thrusts his hands through his hair. "Laura, for fuck's sake, get on the bike."

The rain has completely saturated my coat and down through my shirt, which is now stuck to me.

I'm about to shout *no* at him. Then, the first water drop soaks into my panties, and my resolve begins to fade.

The wetness quickly spreads, and the decision is made. I stalk over to the helmet, snatch it off the ground, and stomp my feet over to the bike, waiting for him.

He throws his hand up and stretches his leg over the bike, sitting down. "Thank God. What's the address?"

I tell him, and he types it into his phone as I settle in behind him. I can't help but giggle at how much I got under his skin.

I place my hands on his shoulders and wait for him to pull off.

He twists, shifting to see me. "Now, I know you're smarter than that. Hold on to me like your life depends on it. Because, well, it does." He turns back around, revving the engine.

Lifting my arms up, I wrap them around his torso, feeling every solid muscle and mound. *Dear God, this boy spends some time on the ice.*

Not a second later, he gives it some gas, and we shoot forward. My arms instinctively tighten, and I can feel him let out a deep breath. My thighs are practically squeezing the life out of his hips.

The air whips around us, and it's refreshing and calming. Definitely needed after that heated argument. It's almost grounding, feeling the wind and the world around us as we ride.

I lean my head against his back, letting myself pretend for a second that this is my life. Alec is my boyfriend; we are going home to our son, and we are in love. That my mom is okay and we aren't swimming in debt. That life is perfect.

I take deep breaths, letting the cool air cleanse me.

As fast as the ride started, it seems to have ended even quicker. We pull into the driveway, and the living room lights are on, letting me know Char is most likely ready to interrogate me when I get inside.

Alec kills the engine and rests the bike on the kickstand, helping me off. Taking the helmet off, I shake some of the mess out of my hair. Which does nothing to the wet strands stuck to my face.

Alec quickly reaches out and swipes them out of the way. "Thanks for letting me bring you home tonight, Lu." He steps back, letting me lead the way to the door.

I hand the helmet over to him. "Thanks for bringing me." I smile at him, trying to keep as much animosity in my tone as I can.

He steps onto the porch and a gentle warm glow is cast over him from the light. Goddammit, his cheekbones are carved out of stone.

He's fidgeting with the helmet when he opens his mouth. "Um, tonight really didn't go as planned. And I still would really like to talk sometime if you're up for it." He glances at the bike.

Regardless of how the night went, we do still need to talk. About a lot of things.

"Yeah."

"Really?" A spark of hope lights in his eyes, and I'd be lying if I said it didn't affect me.

"Yes. Meet me at Nikki's tomorrow at noon. Don't be late."

Without another word, he leans down, and his soft, full lips press the sweetest kiss to my cheek. His kiss grazes the very edge of my lips, and a shiver rolls down my back.

A need and desire I haven't felt in years reignites in my veins.

Ugh. You hate him. You hate him.

He pulls away just enough to speak low into my ear. "By the way, when I was talking about your outfit, I meant that you are the sexiest woman, and in that top and those tight leggings and boots, no man would be able to resist you. Especially me. Good night, Laura. See you tomorrow." He shakes his head as he walks away.

Turning inside, feeling like I got whiplash from how this night has been going.

Walking into the living room, I lock eyes with Charlotte, who is pigging out on a bag of chips.

I head upstairs, mentally exhausted from the day.

"Hey, Laura!" she shouts to me. She doesn't wait for me to respond. "You're fucking welcome."

Y ou ever look at yourself and think something looks off, but you can't figure it out?

Well, I've been in front of this mirror for the last hour, getting ready, trying to figure out what it is. I can't put my finger on it. Rolling my eyes, I officially give up on trying to place it.

I'm meeting up with Alec at Nikki's in twenty minutes. He ended up getting my number from Reed, who had gotten it from Char. I swear this girl is just trying to play matchmaker. It's like she completely forgot that she was there when Alec left in the first place.

Let's just get through this. Then, he can go back to being a professional hockey player, and I can go back to being a mom. How it's supposed to be. How he wanted it to be.

Tomorrow is all about Jack. I've been so busy with my new job and school. I feel like we haven't had a lot of quality time together outside of visiting Mom.

Jack loves to go to the harbor and watch the ships. Whether they are coming in or going out, everything is extremely exciting to him. Personally, I'd rather be home, cuddled up, watching a movie with him, but nothing beats seeing that smile of his.

I pull up to Nikki's and see Alec's motorcycle in the lot already. Hmm, he's early. That's not his usual thing—punctuality.

I walk inside, and Nikki waves at me, lifting an empty cup, now prepping my usual order—a salted caramel cold brew. Alec's back is to the door, so he hasn't seen me yet.

I walk up to the booth and sit across from him. He immediately straightens up, offering a shy smile.

He takes a sip of his coffee. "I would've ordered for you, but I wasn't sure what you wanted." A short laugh leaves his lips. "And after all this time, I couldn't imagine your order is still a salted cara—" He's cut off as Nikki approaches.

"One salted caramel cold brew for my girl." She smiles at me, handing me the cup.

I take the drink, stifling the laugh that wants to escape my lips. Looking up to Alec, I let mine go, seeing he's doing the same thing.

He shakes his head. "I stand corrected."

I nervously tap my fingers on my cup. "Yeah, not much has changed when it comes to my tastes."

His lips instantly tip into that goddamn smirk.

And when I realize what I said, my face instantly heats. *Ugh.*

Were we always this awkward when we were younger?

He blows out a heavy breath. "So, what have you been up to?"

The roller coaster of mood swings from being around him is exhausting. One minute, I forget for just a second what happened between us, and I laugh and smile. Next, I'm fuming when my memory returns.

He must sense the anger boiling beneath the surface because seriousness shines in his eyes. But he waits for me to respond.

He doesn't deserve any details about our perfect son. So, I guess that leaves just one thing.

My eyes drop to my tapping fingers. "My mom's sick, which you already know."

"Oh, Lu." He reaches across the table, his fingers inching closer to mine.

Images of my mom, cold and pale, flash through my mind over and over. But I'm yanked back to reality the second his fingers graze mine.

I immediately pull away from his touch. I'm too vulnerable right now, and that is no place for him. My eyes shoot to his, which are full of … regret?

He folds his hands together. "I'm so sorry, Laura. What happened?"

I lean my head back against the seat and close my eyes, taking a deep breath. My mind is thrown back in time, recounting the endless trips to her hospital room over the last few months. I can still remember it as if it were yesterday. From the details of the cold white room to the mole on the doctor's cheek. It was like my brain was hyperaware the entire time, burning the memories into my mind.

And now, I'm about to relive it all over again, telling Alec. The story never really gets any easier.

"A year ago, she had a hemorrhagic stroke. She wasn't found right away, and by the time I did, she had already gone a long time without oxygen." The backs of my eyes begin to sting, but I push it away, afraid that once I start, I won't be able to stop.

Alec keeps quiet, giving me my time. He's always been annoyingly respectful.

I continue on, pushing past my pain. "By the time she arrived to the hospital, she had to go into surgery—she had bleeding in her brain. She was supposed to wake up right after the anesthesia wore off. But she never did; she still hasn't." I don't realize how low my voice got until I am done.

When I finally find the courage to look up, his eyes are wet, echoing the pain I feel. This time, when his hand reaches out to mine, I let him take it.

"Laura, I'm so sorry. Lisa's strong; she'll pull through."

Blowing out the air I was holding, I respond, my voice still low, "Yeah, she has to."

His thumb strokes over my knuckles, calming my racing heart. As much as I want to, it's hard to hate him right now.

Enough about me. This vulnerability is making my skin crawl. "What about you? How have you been?"

His thumb brushes over my knuckles again, grabbing my attention to it. My brain is begging me to pull away, to cut this off. But I'm afraid it's the only thing holding me together right now.

He continues the soothing movements over and over. "Well, I got signed to the Nighthawks last year. I got a five-year contract with a good salary. It's been great." He looks guilty, probably feeling bad that he doesn't have any new baggage to add.

I lift my thumb up, wrapping it over his thumb, offering a genuine smile. "That's great, Alec. It really is."

Maybe all of this was for the best. Maybe he never would have gotten this far if he had stayed with us. Maybe this all happened the way it was supposed to.

He returns my smile, his dimple popping out. "Thanks, Lu."

I want to hate him. I want to hate every part of him. But he's living his dream. He got everything he'd ever wanted. I can't hate that. No matter how much I want to. A part of me will always love Alec.

Alec clears his throat, pulling my attention back to him. "Can I see you again?"

I pull my hand back, resuming the nervous tapping. I want to walk away. We've been around each other for less than an hour, and I already know that when I leave, I'm going to miss this, miss our connection.

I should say no. But the only word that falls out of my mouth is, "Yes."

His eyes light up, and he lifts his lips into that fucking smirk. "Tonight?"

A laugh slips from my lips. "That was fast."

"Well, why waste any time? And the hockey team's having a party tonight. I'm pretty sure Reed is bringing Charlotte. And I would like to bring you."

His cheeks heat up a little, and I bite my lip at his reaction, shocked I can still cause it.

At least if Char is there, then I'll have an escape goat if I need one. "Okay."

"Okay?" The question huffs out of him, like he is so shocked that I said yes.

"Yes, I'll go with you. What time, and what should I wear? Like, is it dressy?" Suddenly, anxiety floods me. *Ugh, I'm not ready for this.*

"Wear whatever you're comfortable in. And I'll pick you up at eight." He stands, tossing his cup in the nearby bin.

I follow him to the door, which he holds open for me. "Thank you."

He turns, walking backward. "I'll see you tonight, Lu."

With that, he spins, leaving long-lost butterflies fluttering around, anticipating tonight.

I wish we could pretend, pretend that this was our life, that tonight was just another date. That we could just pretend this didn't have an inevitable timer, an inevitable end.

"Lu, hurry the fuck up!" Char shouts from her bathroom.

I look at the murder scene of my closet, still indecisive on what I want to wear. I've gone through practically every possible combination of my jeans and tops.

Char knocks, coming in without a response. "Lu, it's seven fifty. Why aren't you ready ye—oh my fucking God, what happened in here?" Her eyes scan over the piles and piles of clothes strewn on my floor.

I'm sitting on the ground, amid the wreckage. I look up to her with puppy-dog eyes. "Help."

Char breaks into laughter, and it's contagious. After a second, I can't help but join in with her.

I chuck the nearest shirt at her. "Stop it and help me!"

Really looking at her for the first time right now, I realize how freaking great she looks. I lean back on my palms, obnoxiously checking her out. Like her ego needs a boost.

"He-he." She twirls and strikes a ton of poses. "All right, babe, get up. Let's find you an outfit."

She walks over to me and puts her hands out. I take them, and she pulls me up.

With the amount of wardrobe changes she puts me in, we could make a movie montage. After I try almost every shirt on in my closet, Char storms off into her room, coming back with her arms behind her back, the biggest smile on her face.

"Here, this is it. No changing. Let's go." She thrusts a midnight-blue top at me and pushes me into the bathroom.

Getting a good look at it for the first time, I realize it is not a top.

I step into the shimmery, deep-cut, long-sleeved deep-blue surplice bodysuit. Zipping my jeans back up after changing, I take the first look into the mirror, and I don't think Charlotte's ever getting this back.

The front is draped into a super-low V. This will definitely draw attention. I spin to look at the back, which is sheer and crisscross.

Yeah, she's not getting this back.

I flip my head down and shake my hair out, fluffing the curls up before walking back out in the room.

Charlotte whistles, cheering me on, "Yes, yes, yes! Let's go. The boys are outside."

My heart immediately jumps to my throat. I grab my thigh-high black boots and slide them over my ripped black jeggings, and then I follow Char down the stairs.

We quickly say our goodbyes to Jack and Josh before heading to the door.

My chest is tight and keeps getting tighter with each step we take, and by the time we get to the front door, my lungs are burning.

When the door finally opens and the crisp air fills my lungs, the pressure starts to lift.

I look up, and my gaze instantly locks with Alec's.

He straightens up and begins striding toward me, wetting his bottom lip. "You look incredible."

I press my lips together, my eyes dropping to the black T-shirt stretched across his chest. "Thank you. Not so bad yourself."

He smirks, exposing that damn dimple, and slides his leather jacket down off his shoulders. "Here. It'll be cold during the ride."

He holds the jacket up for me to put my arms through. The second it's on, I'm engulfed in him, in the scent of my past, our past. It's so weird to be here, going to a party together after all this time.

He walks off, heading to the bike. Turning his head, he calls to me, "Ready?"

Without a word, I catch up to him I look over, and Char and Reed are in his car, waiting for us.

Throwing my leg over the bike, I grab on to his shoulders, settling down onto the seat. It's not any less awkward this time around. I hesitantly wrap my arms around his waist.

He grabs my hands and pulls me tighter up against him, crossing my arms. Every part of me is pressed up against him. I'm so thankful he can't see my face right now.

He revs the engine, and we take off, Reed's car close behind. But Reed speeds up, and flies by us. The air is whipping all around us, and I'm so thankful he gave me his jacket because, jeez, I was not prepared. But he has to be freezing his ass off.

I shout over the roaring air, "Are you cold?"

He turns his head slightly, and his cheek presses against my forehead. "Laura, with your arms on me right now, I think I might catch fire."

Okay, now, I'm ecstatic he can't see my face.

We ride the rest of the way in silence, and when we pull up to the house, my jaw drops. This is the house some of the team is renting for their stay? It's absolutely breathtaking.

There are endless cars out front, and I'm suddenly getting nervous again. I didn't think it was going to be quite this large of a party. Music is pouring out of the house.

Alec pulls into the driveway and parks next to a car, killing the engine.

He leans the bike against the kickstand and helps me get off. "Ready to go in?"

I immediately look around for Char, but I don't see her anywhere. Turning back to Alec, I realize I only have one option unless I want to be out here alone. "Yes."

He runs his hand behind his neck and smiles at me. "Thank you for coming with me tonight, Lu. It wouldn't be the same without you here." His smile morphs into a smirk. "And I've got the prettiest woman here."

I purse my lips playfully. "Well, you haven't 'got' me, for one. And you haven't seen all the girls here yet."

He doesn't hesitate a second. His eyes are boring into mine when he says, "I don't have to see the other girls here to know you're the most beautiful one, Lu."

My cheeks burn with his words. "Thank you."

"Just a fact."

He holds his hand out, and for once since he's been back, I don't sit and question everything. I just do what I want. And I slide my fingers into his.

When we walk into the house, people turn and look at us, their eyes dropping to our hands. We round the corner, and I finally find Char and Reed, who are talking to Cam.

He turns, as if sensing our presence, and his eyes slowly trail down to our linked hands. He shakes his head ever so slightly, and I wonder if anyone else noticed.

I feel Alec stand a little taller next to me and can't help but laugh at his sense of protectiveness. Nothing has changed since high school.

We finally reach them after wading through the seemingly endless crowd of people.

Char has a drink in her hand, and I think I could use one right about now. I don't have to worry about Jack tonight since he's at home with Josh, so I can cut loose a little bit.

I release his hand and walk up to her. "Get me one." I drop my eyes to her cup.

She nods her head, and without a word, she links her arm through mine and starts leading me away.

But Cam reaches out and catches my arm. "Hey, Laura. Nice seeing you, as always."

I smile up at him. "You too, Cam. Need a drink?"

He looks down at his cup, which is almost full. "Yeah, I could use a new one." He smirks and follows Char and me to wherever we're going.

We end up in the kitchen. The counters are stocked full of bottles of every kind of liquor. Char grabs a cup and starts mixing something up for me. After she is happy with her concoction, she hands it to me, and by the smell, I don't think she mixed the alcohol with anything.

I take a few drinks, and, oh dear God, it's awful. *Let's just get this over with.* I tip my head back and down the rest of the red Solo.

Char turns back around to me and gasps, reaching out for my drink. "Oh my God! Laura! Did you just drink this whole thing?" she shouts at me, her eyes wide.

He-he. I giggle in my mind. "Yeah, so?"

She studies me for a moment before responding, "So, you just drank, like, six shots of vodka, you fuckin' lightweight. You're about to be on your ass."

I laugh in my mind again.

"Oh my God, she's already there. She's a drunk giggler. Can't help herself." She looks at Cam.

I look at her, shocked. "Wait, how could you hear that?"

She looks at me like I'm the biggest idiot in the world. "Because you're laughing."

"Yeah, but in my head." This time, I laugh out loud.

"No, you dumbass, it was not in your head." She bursts out laughing.

She takes back off to the living room, and I follow her, trying to keep my steps in a straight line.

When we round the corner, red floods my vision. Wow, this drink hit me fast. Across the room is Alec, and leaning against the table a foot away from him is this jaw-fucking-dropping beautiful blonde who is trying to pop her boobs out of the top of her shirt by how hard she's pushing them out.

I shouldn't be mad. He's not mine. I'm not his. On top of that, he has his own life, and I have mine. Whatever we are playing at right now, walking down memory lane, it isn't real. We aren't together, we aren't anything. We're two people who showed up at a party together.

He's the one who chose this life over us. He can go fuck himself for all I care—or the blonde for that matter.

I turn around and grab Cam's drink, tipping it back, pouring the liquid courage down my throat. I toss the cup on the table next to us and grab his hand, dragging him to the bodies of people dancing in the room.

"Laura, as much as I want to dance with you right now, I'm not so sure it's a good idea." His eyes are darting behind me.

I walk backward, continuing to drag him with me.

"Come on, Cam. You don't have to worry about Alec. I don't want to dance with him right now, I want to dance with _you_." I bit my bottom lip.

I'm not a complete bitch using Cam to make Alec a little jealous. I know for a fact that I am going to enjoy dancing with Cam. And all it takes to convince him is for me to run my hands down his chest, hooking my fingers in his belt loops, and pulling our bodies flush together.

His smile is stretched ear to ear. "Wow" by Zara Larsson is blaring in the speakers, setting the rhythm of our hips.

He grabs my hip, squeezing tight. I spin in his grasp, grinding my ass against him. We continue to grind and dance.

With the alcohol completely flooding my vision and mind right now, everything's fuzzy, even my anger.

The song gets to the last chorus, and Cam shoves me hard. I turn around, confused as fuck. But Cam isn't standing. He's on the ground, and Alec's on top of him, smashing his fist into Cam's jaw.

I immediately reach out and grab Alec, trying to yank him off of Cam. "Alec, *stop!*" I shout at him over the music.

I grab Alec's attention enough just for Cam to swing back and pop Alec's jaw.

Having had enough of this dumbass macho brawl, I do probably the stupidest thing. I dive between them, but it works. They stop immediately, Alec mid-swing.

He turns to me, and pure fury is in his eyes. His chest is rising and falling rapidly.

I grab his arm. "Outside now."

He hops up and storms off without a word. I get off the ground and follow after him.

Cam reaches out, grabbing my wrist. "Laura, wait."

My veins are hot right now. I snap at him, "What?"

"He's hot. You need to let him cool down." Cam warms, wanting in his eyes.

I care for Cam, I do. And I may have gone a little far tonight using him to make Alec jealous. But I don't have a choice in the matter, it will always be him.

But the fact that Cam's grasp is still tight on my wrist is starting to piss me off. I try to free myself but he doesn't budge. I squint at him and feel a weird calm wash over me. "You know what I need, Cam? I need men to stop controlling my fucking actions." Wow, this alcohol has a mind of its own. "I need *you* to let go of my damn wrist. I've known him since I was fifteen fucking years old, Cam. I know how to handle him. I don't need a lesson from you." Without another word, I yank my wrist out of his grasp, taking off after Alec.

The cool air slaps me in the face when I open the door. I frantically search for him, my vision getting fuzzier and fuzzier by the second.

I race down the driveway and into the street, spinning every way, trying to find his face. Frustrated and angry, I pace back up the driveway. I reach for the handle of the door.

"Laura," Alec calls to me, tension in his voice.

I turn and am rushed with so many feelings. Anger with him for entertaining the blonde, anger with myself for reacting the petty way that I did, and more anger with myself that all I really want to do right now is jump into this man's arms and ask if his face is okay.

What in the hell is wrong with me?

He walks up to me. "What the fuck was that in there?"

I rock back on my heels. "Are you serious right now? How about the blonde whose boobs were practically on your damn face? Huh?"

He throws his hands up. "She was talking to me, not grinding on my fucking dick! You come with me as my date and then go whore out with one of my teammates? Nice, Lu. Real nice. That's not the Laura I know." He scoffs at me.

I laugh. If I thought I saw red before, boy, was I wrong.

I stalk up to him and push his chest. I jut my finger in his face. "Never—and I mean, *never*—call me a whore. You have zero claim on me, Alec. *None!*" I keep taking a step forward, backing him up. "You left to follow your precious dreams. Well, congrats. You *fucking* made it. You got the money and the luxuries. And it looks like you even got the girls. You get to live care free, worry free for no one else in the world except for yourself."

His back is against the garage now, but I wish I could push him through the damn wall. Somewhere behind me, I hear Charlotte call my name.

But I don't let up for a second. "This is the life *you* wanted. You chose this over us. You left *us*. And I was left to pick up the pieces and survive. You don't know me, Alec. You *knew* me. I am nowhere near the girl you left. So, go enjoy your precious life and leave us the hell alone. He's doing great, by the way, not like you've asked."

I shove him once more and storm off to Charlotte.

But not before he shouts back, "What the hell are you talking about, Laura? You broke up with me!"

I ignore him. I'm not fifteen. I refuse to play games with him.

Reed is in his car, waiting for me. Charlotte is holding the door open, and I barely make it into the backseat safely.

"Hey, Alec!" Char shouts. "Go *fuck yourself*!" She slides in and slams the door behind her as Reed takes off.

My blood is boiling. I press my cheek against the cold window and close my eyes.

I should have known better. I did know better. I just didn't care.

I won't make that mistake again.

11

Dear Alec,

I miss you. I miss your hugs. Your smile. Your laugh. I miss you tickling me when I'm sad, just to make me smile. I miss you leaving love notes in my locker. I miss you hiding and watching me open them. I miss pretending I didn't know you were there.

We should be together, Alec. We belong together.

The way I ended things, I didn't want it to happen. I didn't mean for it to happen. All the wrong words came out. And when you pushed back, I didn't know what to do. You fought for us, and I stayed silent. I was scared I was holding you back from your dreams, that I was getting in the way. I knew you wouldn't break up with me for it, so I did what I thought you deserved—to have the world. And hockey will get you there. I believe in you so much. I always have, and I always will.

But you don't need to chase them alone. And I'm so sorry for ending things. I didn't stop loving you. I never will.

I love you more than a hockey player loves the ice. I love you more than I ever thought possible.

I can't love without loving you.

Please forgive me.

But that's only one of the reasons I wrote this letter.

If there was a time for a pause, for the words to get stuck in my throat, it would be here.

Alec, I'm pregnant.

Ten weeks.

You deserve to know that we're having a baby. It's too early to tell if it's a boy or a girl, but either way, I'll love him or her. And I know you will too.

I want us to be together. I want us to be a family.

But I won't force you to do anything you don't want to do.

It's up to you.

Call me, text me, FaceTime me, email me, snail-mail me—I don't care.

I'm waiting.

I love you, always.

Laura

"Just one more, please!" I beg Jack as he poses in front of our porch with his brand-new backpack hanging off his shoulders.

He rolls his eyes. "Moooom!"

I hurry and snap a few more as he throws the cutest little tantrum.

"Okay, okay. Let's go. I don't want you to be late for your first day."

Char and Josh come out of the front door of our house right as I'm helping Jack into his car seat.

My chest is about to explode. I am so grateful for the two best friends in the world. And I am in such shock that my little boy is starting school.

And in that moment, I can't help but think of Alec. Of all the firsts he has missed and will never get to see.

A part of me aches for the missing piece in Jack's life. But at the end of the day, I sit up straight and smile. Because in my mind, I never had a choice to walk away. The second I knew I was pregnant, I was all in.

I try my best to give Jack everything he needs. He never wants for food or clothes or a roof over his head. And I believe that I love him enough to fill the missing piece that is Alec.

As we pull into the school parking lot, the biggest lump forms in my throat. My little baby is starting school. I find the nearest parking spot and shove back the tears building in my eyes.

I get out of my side of the car, walking around to his side, and open his door, helping him out.

He adjusts his backpack on his shoulders and then reaches his little hand up to mine. "You ready?"

My heart clenches. *Am I ready?*

That's my little Jack, always looking out for me.

We walk in silence into the school and follow the colored arrows on the ground to his classroom. Kindergarten class two is the blue arrows.

When we walk into his room, my chest tightens. I'm not ready for my little boy to grow up and be a kindergartener.

I look down to Jack, who's taking in his surroundings, not looking fazed in the slightest.

A little boy across the room waves at him, and Jack smiles and waves back with the biggest smile on his face.

He turns to me and tugs my hand, pulling me down to my knees. "Mommy, it'll be okay."

The well of tears I'm holding back breaks, and a loose tear falls off my eyelashes and travels down my cheek.

Jack reaches out and wipes the tear away. Which only makes me want to cry more.

I pull him against me, hugging him tightly. "I love you, buddy."

And he replies with the line he always does, "Even in the rain?"

I kiss the top of his head. "Even in the storm."

12

After a couple of hours working on my project for The Crooked Spine, Jack barges into my room. "Moooom, hurry up, or we're going to be late." He tackles my knees, wrapping his small arms around my legs. "Come on!" He tugs me.

I push my arms through my sweater and chase him downstairs. He quickly puts on his Spider-Man light-up shoes and heads out the door without a coat. I roll my eyes, pulling a coat for him and a coat for me out of the closet, and then we take off.

The drive to the harbor is pretty short. Oohs and aahs are pouring out of him when we approach the viewing dock. His excitement never wavers, no matter how many times we come. It's been too long since the last time we were here.

"Mom, look!" He jumps up and down, pointing to the giant vessel in the water. He audibly gasps when the bridge begins moving.

I can't help but giggle at his excitement. Children are the purest form of joy—the world hasn't tainted them yet.

Jack and I spend another hour or two watching the ships go in and out, just letting the world move around us.

But we have to leave around seven because Char and I work tonight. The theme is witches, and I'm going to need time for the makeup look I have planned.

Hopefully, it's not too late of a night though because Jack's parent-teacher conference is tomorrow morning at seven thirty. I couldn't make the scheduled evening ones last week because I had work. But his teacher offered to have me come tomorrow morning, and I couldn't really say no.

I'm a little nervous. She said that she needed to talk to me about something, and I haven't really been able to get that phrase off my mind since she said it.

I'm excited to see Callie, Hannah, and the boys. With how emotional this week was, I feel like I haven't seen them in forever.

Jack and I head back to the house soon, and before I know it, Char and I are walking out the door and heading to Fireflies.

We end up getting there pretty early, finishing the prep before anyone else even arrives. They are ecstatic when they see it all done and ready to go. Tonight is the first night that Char and I can fully serve. We know the menu front and back, and we're ready.

The first group I mix for is really simple. They just order eight Scooby Snack shots. I add the rum and whipped cream and slide the platter across the bar to the man who ordered. He winks at me, slides me four twenty-dollar bills and grabs the platter.

The entire night, we are swamped. I literally have no idea how they kept up with orders before Char and I could help.

The benefit of being nonstop busy is that time flies by. When we clock out, I feel like I just clocked in. Except now, I'm five hundred and fifty bucks richer. Not too shabby.

The drive home is a blur. I'm exhausted to the core. It's not like I got a lot of sleep last night.

When I got home from the party, I considered punching a wall. Not my finest moment. I held myself back. I was not going to let Alec have that kind of control over me. Ugh, just thinking about him is boiling my blood all over again.

I wring my hands on the steering wheel, my knuckles whitening from the pressure. Char is already passed out next to me in the car. I slap her thigh when we finally pull into the garage.

She shoos my hand away. "Five more minutes."

I slap her thigh again. "Char, you're sleeping in my car right now. Get the fuck up." I nudge her shoulder.

She slowly rocks awake, opening her eyes. "Oh my God, I feel like I got stoned. Not the drug, like a medieval stoning. Every muscle in my body hurts. Who knew this could be a workout?"

I drag my feet, following her up the stairs. I don't even take my costume off. I fall into my bed, money in hand, and sleep the hardest I have in a long time.

The alarm blares from my phone. Oh my God, I could've sworn that I just lay down. The second alarm comes through not a minute later.

"Ugh."

I shut the alarm off and throw my comforter as far away from me as I can manage. It's too tempting. And I cannot be late to Jack's conference.

I don't have to look good for this, right? At least, not that good. I have never had less motivation in my life.

Why couldn't we just do this over the phone? That would have had the same effect.

Quickly getting ready, I throw jeans and a decent shirt on. I slip flats on my feet and make sure he is up and ready to go.

I must have the best son in the entire world. He is already dressed with his backpack, and he's eating a granola bar in the living room. Like he's just been waiting for me the whole time.

I walk over and give him a small kiss on his head, breathing in my personal scent of happiness. "You ready?"

He hops off the couch. "Yep. Hey, I want to ask you something when we get in the car."

We begin making our way out to the garage.

"Just ask me, bud."

He shakes his head and opens his door, hopping into his car seat. "Not yet."

Impatient, wanting to know what he's being so weird about, I hurry up, buckle him in, and then get in the driver's seat.

Pulling onto the road, I finally break the silence. "Okay, what did you want to ask me, buddy?" I switch between looking at him and watching the road.

He's bouncing his thumbs on top of each other, obviously a little nervous. "I, um … well, I want … I want …" He huffs out a breath.

"Just ask me, buddy. It's okay." My heart tugs at his nerves. I can't imagine why he would be nervous to ask me something.

He keeps playing with his thumbs. "I kinda wanna play a sport."

My smile beams at him through the mirror. "Jack, that's great. What sport?" I try to reassure him the best I can.

"I was talking to Erick because he plays. And he said it's kind of expensive. That's why I'm so nervous to ask. Money's hard, I know. I hear you, Josh, and Char talk sometimes …" He trails off.

My eyes sting. I never want our financial strain to ever hold him back. And since I've started at Fireflies, money has been my least concern.

I stretch my hand back, reaching for his. He takes hold of it.

"Listen, bud, we are doing just fine, okay? You name the sport you want to play, and we will find a way to make it happen, I promise." I give his hand a little squeeze.

His legs begin kicking. "Really?" I can hear the smile in his voice.

I pull into a parking spot at the school and turn, giving him my full attention. "Really, Jack."

His smile is beaming, lighting up my whole world. I grab my water bottle and take a drink.

He shouts, overwhelmed with excitement, "Awesome! I want to play hockey."

I begin choking, spitting the water out of my mouth. *You've got to be kidding me. Could've been dance, football, soccer, basketball—literally anything else. But this boy of mine wants to play hockey?*

I'm not going to let my own issues with a hockey player stop my son from playing the sport he wants.

I shake my head, laughing at the universe's sense of humor. "All right, bud, hockey it is."

With a smile stretching his face ear to ear, we walk into the school hand in hand, and he drags me to his classroom as fast as he can.

Jack is digging in his cubby when his teacher, Ms. Jaime, goes over his recent behavior and schoolwork.

Her voice is sweet, almost like honey. But boy, I would be lying if I said it wasn't full of judgment. "He's a bright boy. And a great student."

I can feel a *but* coming.

"But"—*there it is*—"he just always seems distracted and acts out during lessons. And sometimes, he has a hard time listening. I thought maybe something could be going on at home?" She tilts her head to the side, pretending to be genuine.

I bite the inside of my cheek to refrain from snapping at his teacher. "No, nothing out of the ordinary is going on. I will talk to him about being more respectful during school. Is that all?" I sit back, squeezing my hands together, maybe a little too tight.

She sighs. "There is one more thing." She pauses. "You're aware of his friendship with Erick, right?"

"Yes," I reply, wondering where in the hell this could be going.

"Okay, good. Well, I've been noticing little things between the two of them. They've been sharing snacks, and occasionally, I have caught them holding hands under their desks. Now, I know you're a single mom."

Oh, she'd better watch the next words that come out of her mouth.

She continues as I cut moon shapes into my palms, "But I think Jack could benefit from some masculinity. Maybe joining basketball or football?"

I swear I'm trying to be nice. But I have a really hard time when negative things are said about my son. Now, I didn't know that he and Erick might have a little relationship, but why in the fuck does she think that it's any of her concern?

Her tone of voice is about to meet my hand in five seconds.

She's his teacher. She's his teacher.

I look her dead in the eyes. Putting on my best customer-service voice, I say, "Ms. Jaime, thank you so much for bringing this to my attention. We actually just signed him up for hockey today."

She sits back like she has accomplished what she wanted. "Oh good. I'm glad to see that he's going to get some good boy time—outside of his *friendship* with Erick." She says the word *friendship* like it's poison.

I'm going to slap her.

"Oh, I didn't finish."

Her mouth drops open slightly.

"Jack will be in hockey, but that doesn't change a damn thing about his *friendship* with Erick." I stand up from my seat, looking down at her. "Let me make one thing clear with you, Ms. Jaime. I don't give a flying fuck if my son kisses Erick in your classroom or confesses his love to him. I don't give a fuck if my son wants to wear a skirt to school. He doesn't own a skirt, but if he came home, wanting to, we would drive straight to the mall. And if anyone gave him a dirty look, I would say the same thing I'm about to say to you. Keep your judgmental-ass views away from my perfect son. His happiness isn't hurting yours. So, leave it the fuck alone. And if you have any problems with that, we can continue this conversation with the principal and the school board. I'm sure they would love to hear all about it." I turn and walk over to Jack, picking him up.

She finally rises from her seat, her face burning red. "Where do you think you're going, Laura? We aren't done here."

I scoff at her. "I'm taking Jack dress shopping. I'd offer to grab you something, but I wouldn't want to offend your delicate tastes."

And with that, I escort my son to the office and check him out for a personal day. There is no way in hell I'm leaving him with that woman for another minute without talking with him.

I buckle him into his seat and then hop up next to him, still sitting in the school parking lot. "Jack, look at me."

He turns, and his eyes are scared. But he stays quiet.

"Promise me one thing, okay?"

His bottom lip is quivering, mimicking the shakiness of his voice. "Okay."

The stinging behind my eyes returns. "Promise me that no matter what anyone says or does, you will always be yourself."

He sniffles and hesitates for a moment before saying, "Some kids pick on Erick and me." His little voice shatters my heart.

"No one else's opinion in this world matters but yours. What's in here"—I poke his heart—"this is what's important, okay?"

He doesn't say anything, just throws his arms around my neck, sobbing into me. I absorb every tear of pain, feeling each one burn into my soul.

After he rids his body of all the pent-up sadness, I offer him the only thing I can think of to cheer him up. "Want to go ice skating?"

His mouth drops wide open, gasping. "*Really?*" he screams, not even two feet from me.

I laugh. "Yes. Let me call Char and Josh. I'm sure they'd love to go."

And after I call Char, we soon meet up with them at the rink.

Oh my gosh, I haven't been skating in years, not since Alec last took me.

We each get our skates, and I help lace Jack's up. Char and Josh are already on the ice when we get off the ground.

To help give him some balance, I grab one of the walkers for Jack since he hasn't been skating before.

"All right, buddy, careful first step here." I position his hands on the bar as he takes his first step onto the ice.

He can barely contain the smile on his face. "Mom, look! I'm doing it!"

If by doing it, he means that he has both feet on the ice, then yes, he is indeed doing it.

Josh and Char skate up to us.

Josh goes to his other side. "Looking good, little man. Watch your mom. She's practically a pro."

"All right, Jack, watch my feet."

We both pull to a stop before I take my first step forward, showing him how to push off.

"Transfer the weight from your right heel to your toes and push off, keeping your left foot straight. Like this." I kick off with my right foot, showing him exactly what I said, riding the momentum out on my left foot. "See? Now, you try."

Jack's face is all business when he looks down to his feet. "Okay."

He bends his knees, shifting his weight to his right foot and then transferring it back to his left as he pushes off.

We all clap for him.

"That was perfect. Now, do the same thing but with the other foot."

He does as instructed and begins to transfer back and forth, back and forth. And after a few minutes, he is gliding on the ice all on his own.

Wow, he's a natural. Can skating skills be genetic?

Char, Josh, and I follow closely behind him while he skates. After the first couple laps around the rink, he wants to ditch the walker.

I'm a little hesitant since it's his first time out here, but he really is incredible. And I don't want to hold him back.

"All right, buddy, if you fall, it's okay. It might even hurt a little bit. But you will get up, dust it off, and try again."

I grab the walker from him, and he does what he's been practicing, kicking off and transferring his weight.

I don't think he even needed the walker to start with. He's absolutely brilliant. Like he was born to skate. I'm lost in awe that I barely even register Charlotte's voice.

"Laura," she says matter-of-factly, her tone a warning.

I turn to her, and she's pointing off the ice, near where Jack's skating. And my heart drops.

Alec and a few guys on his team just walked in and are heading for the entrance, right where Jack is about to be.

Oh God, I didn't want their first meeting to be today, if ever.

I dig my blade in and take off, grinding my toe into the ice, flying between skaters, heading straight for Jack.

Alec's laughing with Cam. They haven't seen me yet.

I get to Jack, and Charlotte and Josh are a little behind me. I don't need to use my words to tell them to get him out of here.

Charlotte and Josh take Jack and skate away.

Alec's on the ice by the time I turn back. He's definitely noticed me now, frozen in place.

I fly across the ice, barreling right to Alec, trying to make some kind of distraction so they can get Jack out of here. If and when Alec and Jack ever meet, it won't be the same day that he cried in my arms about his boyfriend.

Alec shakes his head, wearing a hell of a shiner from Cam. His anger from that night seems to have faded. "The ice still suits you, Lu. Look, I want to apologize about the other night. I shouldn't have overreacted. Just seeing you in another mans arms made me murderous. But I shouldn't have taken that out on you."

Holy shit, I have no time to process that right now. I'm so out of breath that I think I might faint. "Alec, can we talk later? I'm heading home right now." For a brief second, I stare into his eyes, "I didn't handle it the best myself. But I should probably go."

Every cell in my body is begging me to turn around and see if Jack is gone, but I can't give it away that I know Jack at all.

Suddenly, Jack's voice cuts through the cheers and shouts in the room. "I don't want to go. I want my mom!"

I don't turn.

Alec breaks my gaze and looks to the noise, to the boy he doesn't know who just wants his mom—wants me.

I hear Josh. "She'll be out in a minute, bud."

Alec's head cocks to the side.

Oh no.

Jack shouts, and I hear Josh shriek. I can't help but turn at the commotion. Jack is gliding across the ice toward me, like he's been skating his whole life. I feel so much fear and pride at the same time.

But then my breath halts.

Everything's colliding at once, and there's nothing I can do right now to stop it.

I never wanted them to meet for the first time unplanned. I wanted to talk to Alec about how we would handle it, them meeting. I wanted time to figure it out. But time is running out as Jack glides on the ice.

Maybe Alec will just pretend he doesn't know him, that this is just a little boy that he doesn't want a relationship with.

Jack gains speed, and I suddenly realize we didn't go over how to stop.

My eyes widen as he closes in.

"Jack, slow down!" I shout to him, instinct taking over. I drop down onto my knees on the ice and prepare for impact.

"Mom, look out!" Jack shouts.

Seconds later, he barrels into me, ice spraying around us. I slowly rise, holding Jack in my arms.

When I turn to finally face Alec, he's completely in shock. His face is ghost white, jaw unhinged.

Alec studies Jack, looking over every inch of him like he is trying to decide if what he is seeing is real.

We stand in silence for what feels like forever before Jack breaks it. "Who are you?"

Alec's wide eyes shoot to my face for a moment before he turns to Jack. He clears his throat. "My name's Alec." His voice is disconnected, almost like it isn't him talking.

Jack shoots a hand out. "Nice to meet you. I'm Jack. How do you know my mom?"

Alec's voice is a whisper. "Your mom?"

Alec's eyebrows furrow. "Jack, how old are you?"

"I'm five. My birthday's in a few months. Mom said she's going to throw me a huge party!" He can't contain his excitement.

I feel like I'm going to puke.

Josh and Charlotte approach on my sides, and Jack reaches for her, going into her arms.

Char whispers something to Jack, who turns back to Alec. "Nice meeting you, Alec."

Alec laughs one short, sharp laugh, thick with emotion that I can't quite decipher. "You too … Jack."

They skate off, leaving Alec and me in our own world. I don't know what to say. This wasn't exactly the reaction I had expected from him. It's not like he didn't know I was pregnant. It was clearly stated in my letter.

Alec stares at the ice, his breaths shallow. And ever so slowly, he drops to his knees.

I stand there, frozen. *Why is he acting so surprised?*

When he lifts his eyes to mine, I begin questioning everything. A tear falls onto his cheek, on the cheek of a man breaking in front of me. A man who I have never seen cry.

His voice is scratchy, wrecked with emotion. "Lu …" His voice trails off. He closes his eyes before continuing, "Lu, is that our … is that our *son?*"

I've only ever felt distant from my body a handful of times in my life—when I found out I was pregnant, when Alec left for good, when I got the call about my mom, and right now.

My voice is a world away. "You knew about Jack, Alec. You've known for years. It was your choice not to be in his life."

He stands back up, and this time, he's mad. "Laura! I didn't know I had a fucking son! Are you serious right now? You think that if I knew, I wouldn't have been here every day, with him, with you?"

My body feeds off his anger, manipulating it tenfold. "Yes, I *know* you knew. I left the letter in your mailbox, telling you how sorry I was for breaking up with you and telling you that I was pregnant and that I missed you. You never texted, called, wrote back. What was I supposed to think?"

"What are you talking about?" He runs his hands through his hair, his shoulders sagging. "I-I never got a letter, Laura. If I knew, if I had known, my choice would have been you. It would have always been you. Why didn't you text? Why didn't you call?"

"I was so scared, so young. We used those letters for words that were sometimes harder to say. And fuck I could barely write it on paper. I was terrified, Alec. When you didn't respond, I took that as your answer."

I can see his pain, cut deep into the harsh lines of his face. In the tears pouring down his face. I'm in shock. All the anger and anguish of abandonment I've felt all these years still burrow into my skin, but it wasn't real. And I don't know how to make it go away.

"Alec, I-I don't know what to say."

His hazel eyes continue to water, pain exploding behind them. He places my hands against his chest. "Laura, I swear to you, I didn't know." He sucks in a sharp breath, his eyes wetting. He pulls my head under his chin, engulfing me in his embrace. "If I had known, if I had known you were pregnant, I would have been here every single damn day. I'm so sorry. I'm *so sorry*, Lu."

His chest shakes, and I don't have to look to know more tears are falling. My heart is shattering and stitching back together, over and over, moment after moment.

The tears burst out my eyes, pouring down my cheeks. The sobs shake my body while I'm in his arms, which tighten around me, claiming my sorrow as his own.

We stay there, locked in each other's torment. This feels like a dream, that there's no way this could be true. I'm terrified that when we pull apart, Alec and I will still be just as we've been. But I think, perhaps, I'm more terrified of the truth—that nothing will ever be the same.

Time has faded. I don't know how long we've been here, wrapped in each other's arms. When I finally pull away, my heart aches, torn apart with the what-ifs of our past.

I feel naive that I assumed he knew. How stupid that we've lost all this time, all these memories.

But what if he's only here now because of Jack, not because of me?

I look up, finding his red-rimmed hazel eyes actively searching mine.

"I'm so sorry that you had to do all of this alone. God, Laura, I'm so sorry. I want to know all about him. What's his favorite color? What's his favorite NHL team?" He chuckles, and I smile that he can't help but slip a little joke into the serious moment.

His hands trail down my arms, his fingers finding mine. I continue to smile up at him, so overwhelmed with everything going on.

"It's okay. Jack and I turned out all right."

My phone buzzes, and I pull it out. There's a text from Char.

> *Josh and Jack took the car. I got us an Uber. It'll be here in five.*

His thumbs are stroking over my fingers. "But I'm here now, Lu. I don't want to go anywhere. Is this why you have been so distant since I got here?" His eyes shift, a hidden fire igniting behind them.

My stomach twists. "Well, yeah. I thought here you were, acting so confident and cool, just flaunting the life you built without us. To be honest, it's going to take me a minute to adjust. I've been hating you for years." I laugh, feeling almost embarrassed that all this time apart shouldn't have happened. "But, I don't want you to be here because you feel like you *have* to, Alec. I want you to be here because you *want* to be."

He inches closer to me, his voice lowering. "Laura, if I didn't want to be here with you, I never would have invited you to that party, and I sure as hell wouldn't have picked a fight with Cam. Seeing his hands on you, his body on yours, made me primal. He's lucky that you were there to stop me. Fuck, Lu, I've been trying to get your attention this entire time. When I saw you at Fireflies, I thought about how lucky I had been that I ever got a chance to date a girl as beautiful as you, inside and out. I'm here because the moment I saw you again, I saw nothing else. Then, your gorgeous eyes wouldn't get out of my mind. Your smile is in every dream I have. I can't get you out of my head, but to be honest, Laura, you never really left." He continues to inch his face toward mine, slowly closing the already-short distance between our lips.

His warm breath caresses my lips, inviting them in.

Suddenly, ice sprays all around us, and a teenager takes off, away from us, laughing. Alec involuntarily jerks, wanting to skate after him.

Laughs rattle out of me—maybe from nerves or maybe because my heart and brain are fried and this is the only emotion left.

Alec turns back to me, smiling. His eyes drop to my lips for a second before moving back to my eyes. His voice is clear, confident. "Go out with me."

I scoff. "What?"

He takes my hands again. "I said, go out with me. I want to take you on a date. A real date. Not like the late-night

McDonald's trips we used to take as kids. Like, we both get dressed up, I get us a car, we go to a nice dinner, and maybe we end it with a good-night kiss." He bites his lip as his eyes caress mine. "Definitely a good-night kiss."

My cheeks instantly warm. I know that this is just Alec, the boy I used to love and know. But dear God, he's a lot more now.

He's just in a hoodie and sweats, but he looks like he stepped off a photo shoot. Not to mention, those damn cheekbones, and for fuck's sake, that jawline. I mean, come on, God, spare some of the good parts for the rest of us.

He smiles, those perfect white teeth shining down on me. "So, what do you say, Laura Young?"

I'm still struggling to release all the pent-up anger I've had all these years. It's hard to let that go in a matter of minutes, but it's anger for nothing. He didn't know about Jack. I can't punish him for that. I can't punish myself for that.

I nod my head at him, sucking my bottom lip between my teeth. "What time?"

He doesn't think, just reacts. He reaches out, grabbing my cheeks, and places his soft, supple lips on my forehead, breathing me in. "I'll pick you up at eight."

He leans back, leaving chills in his wake. He takes my hand, intertwining his fingers with mine, and he pushes off, guiding us to the entrance. "Wait, Lu, do you want to bring Jack?"

The conflicting feelings are back. Just because Alec wants to take me on a date doesn't mean we are going to live happily ever after. I need to see how tonight goes before I set Jack up for any level of heartbreak.

"I thought tonight could be just us." I smile up at him, hoping the universe is finally on my side.

We walk up to Charlotte, who looks torn between punching him in the face and hugging him. I guess I have to catch her up on a lot.

Her arms are crossed. She puts her hand out, stopping us, her focus mainly on Alec. "Look, I hope that whatever is going on here lasts. Because that little boy is what makes this world spin. And if you"—she pokes Alec in the chest—"mess this up or hurt her and him, I promise you, I will break your fucking legs so that you'll never be able to skate again."

She backs up, and he opens his mouth to speak, but she cuts him off. "I love Laura. She is my family. But she has one weakness in this world. And it's you. Do not fuck this up, Alec, because I won't be able to handle helping her pick up the pieces. I watched you destroy her once when you ignored her letter, I can't do it again."

He releases my hand, giving Charlotte his full attention. "I'm sorry to you, to Laura, to Jack. I didn't know, Charlotte. I had no idea Laura was pregnant. I never would have left. I can't stop thinking about what I've missed. His first steps, his first Christmas, birthday, everything. And I missed out on all these years with the most amazing woman I've ever met."

My eyes are watery by the time he's done. I inhale a deep breath and slowly blow it out, feeling years of pressure begin to release. I feel like I've been waiting a lifetime for that.

Charlotte purses her lips and then slowly smiles. Her voice is normal when she speaks, the seriousness gone. "Fine. But the offer of ending your hockey career still stands. Just saying."

I step off the ice, joining skate-less Charlotte. My brows furrow when Alec steps off and drops to his knees in front of me.

He begins undoing my laces. His fingers graze my bare ankle when I slide my foot out, and I never knew that an ankle could be so sensitive. Shivers shoot up my leg from the small contact.

He stands back up with the skates in his arms and the biggest smile on his face. He turns toward the main desk. "See you at eight, Lu." He winks and walks away, leaving Charlotte and me with a thousand unanswered questions.

Our poor Uber driver has to sit and listen to us the whole way home. Mostly listen to Char interrogate me and get short answers before the next question is fired away.

Jack is passed out in his bed when we get home, tuckered out from skating. Maybe hockey will be a good thing after all.

Leaning back in my office chair, I push open my laptop and check my email. "Yes!" I whisper to myself.

The email from The Crooked Spine has arrived. I've been waiting for their owner to send me what he is looking for with this marketing campaign. Along with the budget, target audience, et cetera.

I take notes, being as thorough as I can. My smile doesn't fade once the entire time. The second I get done studying my notes, I start some research.

I deep-dive into finding other local bookstores in our area and look into what they're doing for promos and advertisements. Presenting the same kind of setup to The Crooked Spine is probably not a good idea.

After extensive research on bookstores far and wide and probably two hours of deep thinking later, I've come up with my plan for them. Now, I just need to put it into effect.

But that's not happening right now because I have to start getting ready for Alec's and my date tonight. My cheeks are already flushed with anticipation.

The hangers screech on the metal bar as I rifle through my clothes. I have no idea what to wear. I don't know anything about his plans tonight.

Are a dress and heels too much? Should I wear jeans?

"Charlotte!" I scream her name, hoping she will come to my rescue.

My door creaks open.

"I swear you're helpless."

Turning, I throw a shirt at her. "Just shut up and help me!"

She laughs, catching the shirt. "Okay, okay. Calm down, crazy. You have enough clothes to dress an army. We can certainly find something here."

She walks over to the randomly stuffed racks and begins her search. I huff and sit down in the pile of clothes I've already deemed as noes.

She works her way all the way to the back of the racks, where clothes I haven't seen in years live. No hope there.

I lean my head back against the wall and start humming deliriously.

Char scoffs. "Laura, for fuck's sake, get your ass up. We're going to my room. You normally just steal my clothes anyway."

I hop up and follow her, getting ready to just call it a night if we don't find something soon. Her closet and mine are decorated the same—absolutely no order.

She continues her quest of finding me clothes. "So, where's he taking you?"

"I have no idea. That's why I'm stumped on what to wear. I don't want to overdo it, and I definitely don't want to be underdressed."

Ugh, I wish I weren't getting so worked up over this.

This is supposed to be our first date together … again. I want to look smoking hot, show him what he's missed out on all these years.

It's like a lightbulb goes off in my head. I jump up with a newfound energy. "Charlotte! Where's the dress you wore to that frat date night last year?"

She sits there, thinking for a moment.

"Oh my God, come on. Please tell me you still have it!"

It's literally perfect. I was dying to wear it. I've just never had an occasion. This will definitely pique his interest.

Her eyes go wide, and she turns around, digging through the hangers. Seconds later, she squeals and pulls out exactly what I'm looking for.

It's this stunning deep eggplant purple, almost black. The front drapes together, cutting extremely low. The skirt hits just below my fingertips. But the back is my favorite part. It's almost completely open, except for the thin straps crisscrossing and attaching near the dimples in my back.

It's definitely a *show* and not a *tell* kind of dress. But it's not like he hasn't seen me naked before. Just not since I've really filled out.

If his jaw doesn't drop, I'm turning back and going inside.

I rip it out of Char's hand and strip, hastily stepping into it. It fits like a glove—a plus of being the same size as your best friend.

Char squints her eyes. "It's annoying you still look like that after having Jack."

I know she's just hyping me up.

But I will give myself credit. I was in the gym almost every day leading up to Jack's birth. Being healthy and fit with him was my number one priority. And since then, I've been able to maintain my frame and weight.

I've always struggled with insecurities, and that hasn't changed. As thankful as I am that this body created my son, I still have moments where I hate the stretch marks and the loose skin on my stomach.

There's a difference between having insecurities and not knowing your worth. I know who I am. I'm a mother who has worked her ass off to provide for her son and whose mom is in the hospital.

I finish fastening the clasps on my black stilettos and walk over to her, pulling her into a hug. "Love you, Char Bear." I haven't called her that in years. The last time was probably in high school.

She squeezes just as hard, if not harder. "I love you too, Lu Boo."

I can't help but laugh at the use of our old nicknames.

This is such an odd thing, going on a date with my ex. Feelings of nostalgia meld with new nerves and excitement. It's just weird, plain and simple.

I turn, and Char smacks me on the ass.

"As much as I love Jack, please don't make him a big brother tonight."

I turn, scolding her with my mom stare.

She points a finger at me. "That doesn't work on me!"

Grabbing my phone, I slip it into the clutch right after checking the time—7:58 pm.

Here goes nothing.

Jack shouts as I descend the stairs, "Mom! There's a limo outside!"

I swear this boy's imagination will be the death of me.

But when I step in front of the bay window, my jaw drops. A black stretch limousine is parked on the street. And leaning against it is Alec with a bouquet of roses in his hand.

A smile breaks onto my lips. It's a good thing I went with this dress because he's in a suit. And dear God, it might be hard not to make another Jack with him tonight.

Leaning down to Jack, I place a light kiss on the top of his head. "Be good, tonight. I love you."

"I love you too!" He shouts way louder than needed, and I can't help but chuckle.

I grab my black button coat and head outside, unable to keep the excitement off my face.

How is he getting handsomer with each step I take?

He blows a breath out, his eyes shining. He carefully scans my body, studying me like it's the last time he'll ever get to.

When his eyes meet mine again, they are burning, begging to claim me. "I never should have left."

I close the distance between us. Slowly rubbing my hand along his stubbled jaw, I stretch onto my toes and kiss his cheek, making sure I graze the corner of his lips. My eyes close on the impact.

I breathe him in before pulling away. "But you're here now."

He smiles, and that gorgeous dimple sinks into his cheek. "After you."

I slip my hand into his outstretched one as he helps me into the limo. He hands me a glass of champagne and the roses. I take the deepest breath of the fresh floral scent, one of my favorite smells.

Alec hasn't taken his eyes off of me since we got in, and it's a little intimidating. He might be just Alec, but he's also the New York Nighthawks star center and captain. On top of that, he's aged like the finest wine. I'm having a hard time dealing with the fact that this is still *just* Alec.

He reaches over and rests his hand on my knee. Sparks radiate from his touch, like my nerves are catching on fire.

"You're so beautiful, Laura." His words move slower. "So damn beautiful."

I gulp, the best pressure settling in my chest. "Thank you."

His eyes rake over my face, my blush following his trail. He scoots closer to me, sliding his hand into my hair before opening his mouth again. "I want to know everything. I know we *knew* each other, Lu, but I want to know *you* now. The you a year ago, two years ago. I need to learn every moment between now and then—what's changed, what's new. I want to know how to make you laugh and smile. How to make you happy."

My jaw is unhinged when he finishes. I'm at a total loss for words. His hazel eyes are locked on mine.

I lick my lips before whispering to him, "I've missed you."

He doesn't hesitate.

He pulls me against him, and his lips claim mine. I run my hands into his hair and part my lips. His tongue teases mine, and a moan escapes me as his hands tighten in my hair. His tongue continues to explore, and every cell in my body submits to his touch.

A throaty, deep sound rumbles out of him before he abruptly pulls away. He has a look of sadness in his eyes. "I'm sorry. I didn't mean for that to be that, um … intense." He wipes his bottom lip with his thumb, which only makes me want to run my tongue along the same path.

His gaze drops to my chest, ever so slightly stalking up my body and back to my dilated eyes. "And if we don't stop now, I think we're gonna miss our reservation." He smirks.

Emotions well in my throat. Being around him is overwhelming in every way.

"Is this weird?" The question slips out of me before I can stop it.

He furrows his brow and then does something I don't expect. He starts laughing. "I don't know if *weird* is the right word. But it's *interesting*. It feels like we just picked back up, like we never stopped. Or is that just me?" he asks hesitantly.

My smile deepens, and I reassure him, "It's not just you."

Sitting up, he opens the door to the limo, which I didn't even notice had stopped moving.

He turns, giving me his full attention. "I don't want to rush into anything, Lu. I want to do this right. I need to make up for all the time I missed with you. Starting with right now."

He offers me his heart in his hand.

I'm scared. *What if this doesn't work again? I can't handle feeling that pain.*

What about Jack? What about hockey and school?

What-ifs flood my mind, but when I look back up into those golden-hazel eyes, every worry fades to the background.

If he breaks my heart again, it might be the death of me. But not trying would certainly be worse.

I do the only thing I can. I place my hand in his and give him my heart.

"Name, please." The maître d' glances up to us and then back down to his list.

"Kostelecky. I called earlier today." His voice surprises me. It's assertive and full, not like the laughing tone he just used in the limo.

His eyes shoot up, widening. Stumbling over his words, he responds, "Oh, yes, sir. Of course. Right this way."

Alec slides his hand into mine and follows behind the man, giving me a mischievous smile. I squint my eyes at him, wondering what he's up to.

But more than anything, I'm taken aback at how the maître d's demeanor completely changed when he realized who Alec was. His social status is something that I will never get used to.

A couple stands up, heading our way, which forces me to step behind Alec with my hand still locked into his. We pass through a curtained doorway, and I step out from behind him. When I look up, my feet stagger, and Alec quickly drops my hand and steadies me.

When I finally gain my footing, I take in the room. "Ho-how did you do all this?"

Lights are hanging all over from the ceiling, creating the most romantic glow. And the table is set with roses and candles.

He leans in and presses the sweetest kiss to my forehead. "I'm not the same teenage boy I was before. I've got some tricks up my sleeve now, just you wait." He winks at me and pulls my chair out.

Settling into it, I open the menu, trying to keep the redness in my cheeks at bay.

He chuckles, stretching his free hand out. When his eyes find mine, they are engulfed in want and need, fueling the barely controlled blush all over my body.

"I missed you, Lu."

His thumb strokes slowly over my palm, and shivers shoot up my arm.

I smile at him, letting the desire show in my eyes. "I missed you too, Alec. You have no idea."

His hand squeezes mine. "I'd like to find out." He smirks and then runs his tongue over his bottom lip.

The waitress approaches us, and when she notices Alec, she lowers her chin, batting her eyelashes.

Oh God, here we go.

She clears her throat. "What can I get you to drink?" She attempts to sound sexy—annoyingly enough, to any guy in the vicinity, I think she does.

She only looks at Alec, but his gaze hasn't left mine.

"Jack and Coke, please."

She continues to bat her eyelashes at Alec, whose eyes still haven't wavered from mine.

She doesn't even turn to me when she asks, "And for you?" Her tone is annoyed and dripping with jealousy.

Aw, it must be so hard for her.

I look up and wait for her to meet my eyes. A streak of self-assurance hums through me.

When her eyes find mine, I sit back in my seat, forcing her gaze to stay locked on me. Her false confidence wavers.

"I'll have ice water with a slice of lemon, please, and a side of respect. Thank you. That's all."

I turn back to Alec, whose jaw is now on the floor, and he's barely containing his laughter. The waitress sees his giggles and storms off.

His gorgeous hazel eyes find mine, and his thumb continues to stroke my palm. "Laura Young. Tsk-tsk-tsk. You *fucking* amaze me."

I smirk at him, bathing in his compliment.

I know at some point, we need to talk about Jack and figure out how the hell we are going to handle telling Jack that Alec is his dad, what parenting will look like long distance, what Alec and I will look like long distance. But tonight, I want it to be about us, to see if this could even work before we drag my precious baby into it.

Before he can get a word out, I end whatever conversation he might try to start. "Alec, look, I know we need to talk about Jack." I scoff. "We need to talk about a lot of things. But right now, I just want us to be on a date as Laura and Alec. And I want to pretend like nothing else exists outside these walls."

He takes a minute to consider my words. His smile is all the answer I need. "Deal. But after tonight, I want to know everything about him. His favorite color, car, sport, flower. What makes him happy, what makes him sad, mad, giddy, everything."

The intensity of our conversation is cut short as a different waiter brings us the pre-decided appetizer as well as the drinks. Shortly after that, our main course arrives.

The first bite of the New York strip, and I swear I start to drool.

I moan on the second bite, my eyes drifting shut. "Oh my Lord."

When I open my eyes, my breath falters. Alec's gaze is locked on my lips, a roaring fire blazing in his eyes.

My breath hitches and my voice is quiet. "Alec?"

His eyes find mine, slowly sliding up, and I think we might be done with dinner sooner than planned.

His voice is rough when he finally opens his mouth. "Mmhmm. Nothing has changed, you know? You still drive me absolutely fucking crazy, Clumsy."

My voice is barely a whisper as his words smack the air out of my lungs at the use of the long-forgotten nickname. "You remember?"

He smiles, the same dimple appearing on his cheek. "I'll always remember every single thing between us. I remember what you wore that day I caught you falling off the steps. I remember how you sounded on the phone and how my fucking heart would skip a beat when I heard your voice. I remember every detail of our first date and every one in between. My brain erases pointless memories, just to keep the simplest ones with you."

He lifts my hand up to his lips and flicks his tongue on the tip of my index finger, causing shivers to roll through my bones.

It has been far too long since the last time I had sex. The last time was literally when Alec and I conceived Jack. And I am woman enough to own up to the fact that I could use some sex right now.

I sit up, commanding his attention. "Any chance you're not hungry anymore? Want to head back to your place?"

That damn dimple pops out from his smirk, and I would bet money that he's in agreement with me.

He doesn't say a thing. He just stands up and walks out of our private room. He returns not a handful of minutes later, stopping right in front of me. I turn in my chair, swinging my legs around.

His hand wraps around my jaw, settling beneath my ear, and he guides me up and out of the chair.

His thumb strokes my cheek, and he tortures me, ever so slightly bringing his lips closer to mine.

But to Alec's surprise, there is one more thing that has changed about me.

I know what I want, and if I want it, *I take it.*

I slide my fingers into his hair, taking control. Not hesitating for a second, I close the last inch between our lips and guide the way.

I pull his bottom lip between my teeth, and when his deep moan vibrates in my mouth, I swear my clothes try to disintegrate off my body. If my hands weren't locked in his hair, I just might help them off—in the middle of a restaurant or not. I mean, it's a private room after all.

I can tell Alec's getting restless, letting me lead. He is starting to push back more and more with my every move. He never was good at *not* being the captain, no matter the circumstance.

The second I give him full control, one of his hands finds my hip, digging in, and the thumb of his other hand finds the pulse of my neck.

He pulls back, our kiss separating, and he runs his tongue across my bottom lip. My ears start ringing from the blood rushing so fast in my body.

His fingers continue to squeeze my throat as he plunges his tongue back into my mouth, creating a whole new rhythm than we had before; it's faster yet more sensual. His mouth claims me, his kiss seeping into every cell, lighting the nerves on fire.

He leans back. And when he doesn't make another move, I open my eyes, confused. His hand is now wrapped along my jaw, and his other fingers are still curled around my hip.

His voice is throaty and pleading when he says, "Lu, I don't know how much longer I can hold back. Power, control has always been my strength. But you are the one weakness I've always had."

"Fuck." I whisper unintentionally.

He backs us up until my shoulders find the wall, and his hand rounds my thigh, his fingertips trailing up my bare skin.

A finger hitches the lace on my hip. He leans in and nibbles on my earlobe. Warm pulses throb between my legs.

"If we don't leave in the next minute or two, I'm gonna rip your panties off and fuck you against this wall. I don't give a fuck who hears."

His lips graze my jaw as I decide if I'll let him. But dear God, we have already done way too much in a public place. Regardless of it being in a private, closed-off room, it still feels wrong. But somehow oh-so right.

I nod my head, not completely sure what I'm agreeing to.

Suddenly, my phone goes off, blaring my ringtone into the room. I fumble away from Alec, the word *graceful* cut from my vocab.

I grab my phone, and Charlotte's name is illuminated on the screen.

I answer immediately, knowing it will only be about Jack and her calling means she couldn't fix it herself. "Char, what's wrong?"

I hear incoherent mumbling on the other line, and my mom senses tingle.

"Charlotte."

"Lu, I don't know. He's been running a fever and asking for you. And after a point of me saying you'll be home soon, he freaked out and started throwing the tantrum of all tantrums. I have no idea how to get him to stop."

My heart aches for my boy in pain. "Hand him the phone," I order Charlotte.

I hear rustling and then eventually Jack's small voice. "Mommy?"

I sit back down in my chair. "Hey, buddy. I'm coming home right now, okay? Just take a deep breath, and I'll be right there, okay?"

I haven't looked back to Alec yet. I don't want to see the disappointment on his face. But *I* don't come first. My son does, and he always will.

Jack sniffles. "Okay, Mom. I love you."

"I love you too, baby." I smile into the phone.

Not a second later, he says what I was waiting for, "Even in the rain?"

I finish it. "Even in the storm."

I click the phone off and slide it into my purse before I'm ready to face Alec.

But he makes the first move. "Is-is he okay?"

When I look up to him, my heart twists, feeling overwhelmed with emotion. His eyes are full of sadness, racked with concern.

Nodding, I say, "Yeah, it's probably just a cold."

When I stand up, he snakes his hand around my waist.

"The car should be up front." He smiles. "Probably has been for a while. Come on. Let's go check on him."

I follow him to the limo, climbing in behind him. When his hand lands on my knee, it suddenly hits me.

Let's? He wants to come with?

I'm torn. I didn't really even consider the fact that he would offer to join me with Jack tonight. But I don't know if I'm ready for that. But he was also kept out of Jack's life for so many years already. I don't want to make Jack or him miss out on more.

Ugh.

Alec pokes my forehead. "What's going on in there?"

My words fall from my lips before I even realize it. "Jack doesn't know you're his dad. He just thinks that you're his mommy's friend. And I don't want to change that right now. At least, not tonight. Is that okay? If you want to come in. Which you totally don't have to." I cut my ramble off, trying to gather my thoughts.

Alec grabs my face in his hands, pulling my undivided attention to him. "First, I would love to come see him tonight. Second, I am just fine, pretending to be your friend right now, if that's easier on you and him."

I settle into his grasp, my eyes drifting shut.

He straightens my head up, making me open my eyes. "But let's get one thing straight, Lu. I don't want to be your *friend*." He leans down until he's less than an inch from my face, his eyes locked on my lips. "I want to be yours, and I want you to be mine. I want to be the one you turn to. The one to make you happy and to make you laugh. To hold you when you cry. I want to hear my name fall off your lips when I worship you. I want all of it. But I definitely don't want you to ever think that I consider us *just* friends."

My jaw is unhinged when he ends.

Alec really wants that? All of that?

It's terrifying, giving someone your heart again. Especially knowing the pain it causes when it breaks.

But I know that walking away from this, from what's growing between us, would be the biggest mistake of my life. I loved Alec. And I don't know if I ever truly stopped.

I have no words for him to prove that that's what I want too. So, I offer him all I can. "Kiss me."

And fucking hell, he does just that.

The limo comes to a stop, and my heart is pounding, threatening to break through my rib cage. Alec helps me out of the limo, and we make our way up the sidewalk.

I know Jack already met Alec. But this is different. This time, it will be in our house, our home. He's coming to check on Jack while he's sick, vulnerable. The mom in me is saying that this is such a bad idea. That I should tell Alec to go home and that we can try this another time.

But every time is going to be scary. I have to stop living my life on the sidelines. I've been doing it since I had Jack. I sit back and watch all the excitement of life, never being in the middle of it.

That ends today.

Sliding my key in the lock, I think my heart is a beat away from exploding.

The second the door opens, Josh raises his hand, gesturing upstairs.

We quickly walk inside, and I slowly shut the door behind me, locking it. I slip my heels off and look at Alec, who already has his coat and shoes off. His hands are crossed, clasped at his belt.

Rocking back and forth on his heels, he whispers to me, "I can stay here if you want, Lu. Your pace."

If we're going to do this, we might as well go all the way.

"No, I want you with me."

Without another word, I link my fingers in his and lead him upstairs. We pass the guest bath and my bedroom, stopping right outside Jack's door.

I knock once and twist the handle. Before I can even open it, I can hear Jack's pitter-patter to the door.

Jack's sweet voice cracks when he says, "Mommy, you're here!"

He wraps his arms around my legs. He gives me a hug and steps back. When he notices Alec, he tilts his head to the side.

Jack studies him for a moment, and then a lightbulb goes off. "You're the guy from skating."

Alec looks hesitantly at me before bending down to his knees. "Yeah, I am. Do you remember my name?"

Jack abruptly nods his head. I'm afraid he'll give himself whiplash one of these times.

"Yep. Alec. With a *C*, not an *X*." Jack smiles at him, standing up a little straighter.

I'm beginning to suspect that Jack was never really that sick. I reach out to place my wrist on his forehead.

This little shit. He's not even warm.

I join Alec at Jack's level. "How are you feeling, buddy?"

His eyes go wide, and he crosses his hands behind his back. "Better now."

"Mmhmm." I smile at him, slowly shaking my head.

Jack turns his attention back to Alec. "Wanna see my room?"

Alec bites his lip when his eyes lock with mine. "Would that be okay, Laura?"

Jack interrupts, "Mom, pleeeease?"

139

Standing back up, I straighten my dress out. "Okay, okay. I'm going to go change. You've got five minutes."

Jack thrusts his hand in the air. "Yes! Come on, Alec!"

Alec stands up next to me, his eyes finding mine. "Thank you." His gaze drops ever so slightly to my lips, making these damn butterflies flutter again.

"It's no problem. I'll be back in a minute." I point to my bedroom door. "I'll be right in there if you need me."

He turns into Jack's room, whispering under his breath, "I'll always need you."

I'm frozen for a second, debating between letting him know that I heard him and letting him have his moment. Going with the latter, I turn toward my room, completely unable to keep the smile off of my face.

When I get into my bathroom, I reach for my makeup wipes, itching to feel the relief of a bare face. I pull the pins out of my hair, letting the loose curls fall around my face.

I stroll to my closet, almost giddy to get into some sweatpants and a T-shirt. Slipping into my favorite pair of gray sweats, I take my bra off and shove my arms into a rugged, oversize Duluth High Greyhounds hockey T-shirt. As of late, this has been the shirt my hands gravitate toward.

Kicking my feet into my little slippers, I head back to Jack's room. When I open the door to his room, my heart finally bursts. My eyes well up at the perfect sight before me.

Alec is sitting in Jack's tiny car bed, looking like a Doberman in a Chihuahua's dog bed. Jack is curled into his side with his head on Alec's shoulder, fast asleep.

Alec's hand is calmly rubbing up and down his back, so softly that it looks like he's barely touching him.

I remember being like that with Jack at first. Being so scared to harm a hair on his head that every move you make is made with the utmost delicacy.

If you had told me a month ago that I would walk into Jack's bedroom and see Alec holding him, I would have slapped the craziness out of you.

But nothing in the world can compare to the feeling of rightness and the feeling of being whole that this brings.

I whisper to him while making my way to the side of the bed, "Hey."

His eyes playfully scan my body, making me suddenly nervous if I went a little too comfy with my appearance.

He runs his tongue over his bottom lip before biting it. "You look great. Nice T-shirt, by the way." Winking at me, he slides Jack off of his shoulder, tucking him underneath the blanket.

Alec remains there for a moment, just looking at Jack. He stretches his hand out and strokes his thumb across Jack's cheek with the most heartwarming smile on his lips. "Good night, Jack."

He kicks his legs off the bed and rises to take a step. But when he puts his foot down, he finds a Lego and stumbles forward toward me. His other foot slams into the ground as he falls. I reach my hands out to try to catch him. But he's a billion times bigger and stronger than me. When his hands find mine, he continues to crash into me, pushing me back.

My fingers are still locked in his when we fall into the wall, our hands pinned above my head, his lips hovering over mine. It takes all but a second for him to recover from our crash.

His warm breath is teasing me, begging me to make a move. I'm breathing heavily, somehow exhausted. More like panting because his face is an inch from mine and he has my hands secured above my head. His forehead slowly rolls onto mine, his breath matching my pace.

"Laura." His voice is breathy, husky.

Slightly raising my head up, I take a deep breath and step out around him, immediately feeling the loss of his warmth.

I turn back to him with the biggest smirk on my face and whisper, "Come on."

His dimple makes an appearance, and he follows me, avoiding all the Legos this time.

After he passes through the doorframe, I shut the light off and quietly close Jack's door. We move silently to my room, his hand guiding my back the whole way as I lead. When I close my door, the air changes. It's shifting, smoldering, begging to be lit ablaze.

Alec's grip on my back tightens, and in one swift move, he spins me, pulling me flush against his chest. I'm bathing in his warm breath, getting lost in his touch.

Backing us up against my wall, he says, "Lu, you have no idea how much I've missed you."

His fingers find my hairline, and ever so slightly, they trail down my face, caressing me, sending tingles down my neck and spine.

His lips follow his fingers, carefully placing kisses in their path. When his kiss finds my jaw, a small moan escapes my parted lips.

The hand on my back digs in, pulling my hips into his. And oh Lord, his dick has definitely grown since the last time we were in this position.

His kiss continues to drift down my jaw, finding the sensitive spot at the base of my neck.

I give my hands permission to move, and they begin to travel up his chiseled torso. Professional hockey has definitely done wonders for this man's body. I continue trailing my hands upward and wrap them around his neck, deepening his scorching kiss on my skin.

His tongue finds this irregular rhythm that curls my toes into the carpet.

"Alec." His name comes out breathless, desperate.

He pulls away from my neck, returning to his towering height. His fingers tease me, lifting my shirt and sliding over my bare skin.

He slowly leans down, his lips grazing mine. "Tell me what you want, Lu. Tell me, and it's yours."

I look up, finding his eyes are open and locked on my lips, flickering up when he sees my gaze.

Sticking my tongue out to lick my lips, I accidentally graze his. He sucks in a sharp breath, waiting for my move.

"Tell me what you want." His fingers continue teasing me, rising up right beneath my breasts but never going all the way.

He moves them up again, going further than before. His hands freeze, torturing me with what's to come.

"Say it, Laura." His fingers dance back and forth, tightening the already-straining tension in my chest.

"I want …"

His fingers move higher, grazing one of my nipples, forcing me to suck in a breath.

"I want you."

Without a word, he yanks his hands from my shirt, grabs the back of my thighs, and lifts me up, wrapping my legs around his waist.

His lips crash down onto mine. "About fucking time," he growls into my mouth.

His forceful kiss possesses me, branding his name on my heart. He steps forward, sandwiching me between him and the wall. His tongue grazes my lips, begging for entrance. I grant it, and it finds mine like a magnet.

I instinctually roll my hips from the fire burning in my veins. My center presses into the bulge in his pants.

Breaking the kiss, he breathes into my parted lips, "Laura, look at me."

I lift my gaze to his hooded eyes.

"Good girl." He takes slow steps toward the bed. "*Fuck, Lu.* I want to taste every inch of your body." His hips roll against me, and my eyes roll back.

"I want tonight to be about you, Lu. I just want to enjoy making you come, and trust me, I will enjoy it as much as you."

He places his hands on my hips and hooks his fingers in the waistband. In one swift movement, he pulls my sweats down to my ankles and tosses them onto the floor.

His hands find my hips again, his fingers biting at my skin. The roughness of his grip makes me gasp. Which in turn makes him moan.

He hovers over me, his hooded eyes locking with mine. His stare is liquid desire. "Mmm. My dick is craving you so bad, Lu. I want to fuck you until you can't take it, until you're panting, until you come so hard that you can't see straight. And trust me, I will. But I'm going to make you wait. I'm going to make me wait. No matter how hard it is. Because when that time comes, I want you to have no doubts about us. That when neither of us can take it anymore and we finally give in, I need you to know that once I fuck you, there's no going back. There will never again be another girl or another guy. I'm yours, and you're mine." His hot tongue runs up my jaw. "And more than anything, tonight, I want to watch you come with your legs wrapped around my neck."

He bends down and lowers his lips to mine, making me want so much more than what he's going to give.

He begins to kiss down my body. He nips at the peaks beneath my shirt before trailing his lips and tongue down my exposed stomach, giving extra kisses to each stretch mark.

When he reaches the lace on my hips, he looks up to me with primal desire in his eyes. He flicks his tongue on my hip bone, making me jerk in response.

Then, he takes the lace between his teeth and pulls them down my bare legs, the throbbing between my legs begging for his touch.

He tosses the bundle of lace onto the sweats without tearing his eyes off of me. Taking my ankle in his hand, he begins placing delicate kisses, starting at my heel and working toward the most sensitive part of me. Each kiss is getting rougher as he claims every inch of my skin.

When he gets to the edge of my center, I'm bursting at the seams. I didn't know that kisses and nibbles on my skin could feel like this, that it could feel this intense. It's definitely better than my own hand.

His eyes flicker up to me right before his tongue runs up my sex. My head rolls back, my eyes following. Whimpers and cries escape me in a constant rhythm as his tongue circles my clit.

One of his arms hooks underneath my leg, locking me in his grasp. His other hand begins stroking up my inner thigh.

His fingers find my entrance, threatening to throw me over the edge. He pushes two fingers inside, pumping in and out until I'm almost begging for release.

My back arches off the bed, my legs quivering as his pace speeds up. My moans are uncontrollable, at his beck and call.

He pulls his kiss away, and in a rough, deep voice, he orders, "Look at me."

With every remaining ounce of willpower I have left, I lift my gaze up. His eyes are on fire. He's enjoying this just as much as I am.

His pace picks up again, thrusting his fingers into me faster and faster. "Come for me."

I crash, spiraling into the darkness. Shock waves pulse through my core, and I arch my back far off the bed.

"Good girl." Wet warmth latches on to me. Alec licks and sucks like I'm the most luscious drink, lapping me up.

When my body stops rocking from the waves and my breathing begins to slow, he pulls away, stands up, and lies down on the bed next to me.

Feeling way too vulnerable, I lay my hands over my face, shutting my eyes. But Alec grabs them and pulls them away. Finally forcing my eyes open, I look at him, and he's beaming, proud of what he just did.

I shake my head, laughing, overwhelmed with all the emotions coursing in me. But mostly in shock. Because he was most certainly not that good at oral before. If it were an Olympic sport, he would take gold.

He grabs a pillow and lightly hits me with it. "What's so funny?"

I prop myself up onto my elbows and get a good look at him. He has no idea the grasp he has on my heart.

"Thank you for coming over, for being here." My cheeks heat up at the thought of what just happened. "And, well, thanks for that too." I laugh.

He smiles, exposing that damn dimple. "There is nowhere else I would rather be, Lu. And you don't ever have to thank me for that." His eyes scan down my body. "*Trust me,* that was as much for me as it was for you."

There's been a question in my mind since we got here tonight, but I'm scared to ask him. Even after what we just did, it feels like a step. And I don't know if he wants to take it.

"I know that look, Lu. What's up?" Alec's eyes are all serious, homed in one hundred percent on me.

I hate how well he can read me. He's always been able to read me like a damn book.

"I was wondering if you wanted to stay here tonight. It's really late, and I …" I trail off from the excuse I was going to give. "I just want you here, with me."

He takes my hand in his, slowly stroking his fingers over mine. Without a word, he leans over and kisses me. But this kiss is gentle and loving. It's as soft as a feather and as deep as the ocean.

When he pulls away, a sting burns behind my eyes. It's been so long, so hard to do all of this alone.

He kisses my cheek. "I was hoping you were going to ask, by the way."

He wraps me up in his arms, and I feel myself sink into him. All my stress, anger, and pain melt against him.

A peace I haven't felt in a long time settles into my heart.

The dragon nudges my side again.

"Knock it off. Five more minutes." I shoo the beast away with my hand.

It doesn't leave. Instead, it nudges me again. And when I ignore it, it speaks to me in a whispered tone. "Mom, can I lie with you?"

Wow, the dragon sounds a lot like …

Oh my God!

My eyes smack open, revealing a blurry little Jack standing at the edge of my bed.

His eyes keep flashing behind me, and I don't understand until my body recognizes the feel of a warm arm draped over my waist.

Alec.

I wiggle out from under his heavy arm and push myself up onto my elbow. *How in the hell am I going to explain this?*

"Hi, buddy." My voice is hoarse and broken from my deep sleep.

He raises his hand and points to Alec. "Does he live here now?"

My eyes widen. "No, honey, of course not. It was just really late last night, and I didn't want him to drive home."

Jack crawls up into bed and nestles into my arms. "Can he live here?"

My eyebrows furrow, and with my brain just waking up, my words fall irregularly from my lips. "Wh-why would you want that?"

He rolls over, looking into my eyes. "I like him. And he likes my room. It'd be cool."

This is way too much to deal with the second I wake up. I glance at my phone and tap it with my finger. It's six thirty a.m.

Good God, where does this boy get his sleep schedule?

A deep groan sounds behind us, and I can't suppress the giggle in time. Alec hooks his arm around me again, tugging me against his firm chest, pulling Jack with him.

I wonder if he would want to go with us today to see Mom. It's been a long time, and she isn't exactly her best self right now.

Alec is shifting a lot behind me. I've got a good guess he's not sleeping anymore from the growing pressure on my butt.

I clear my throat to get his attention. He sits up on his elbows, and his eyes bulge at seeing Jack.

"Good morning, guys." His voice is thick and raspy.

Jack, full of energy, bursts up. "Good morning, Alec! Can we play with cars today?"

I'm starting to think he didn't come in here to lie with me.

Alec's gaze falls to me before he answers, "Of course. It depends on what your mom has planned though."

Jack's puppy-dog eyes are in full force as he jumps on top of me. "Please, Mom!"

I run my hand over his fine brown hair. "You know we see Grandma on Sundays, Jack. Have you decided if you want to go visit her today?"

"Can I play with cars instead?" He looks up to Alec, and it's an image I thought I would never see.

"Jack, if you don't want to go, you have to stay here with Josh or Char. I'm sure you could play with your cars." I begin to sit up. Jack is reminding me of just how full my bladder is right about now.

"Alec, do you wanna stay and play?" Jack's eyes are locked and loaded right on Alec.

Alec doesn't hesitate. "I thought I would go with your mom to see your grandma today. How about we play later tonight? If that's okay?" He turns to me for permission.

That sense of peace I found last night grabs hold a little tighter with his words.

I lift my hand and rest it on top of his. "That would be amazing."

He adjusts his fingers, giving my hand a little squeeze. "What time are we leaving?"

"We can head there anytime after eight."

He sticks his arms high in the air, stretching. "Can we swing by my place, so I can change?"

"Yeah, of course," I respond while running a hand through my hair—ugh, my greasy hair. "Would you mind hanging with Jack while I shower?"

I bite my lip, hoping it isn't too much to ask. I know he said he wants to be here, but it's still new.

He smiles, exposing that damn dimple. Winking at me, he says, "I would love to." He turns his attention to Jack. "What do you say we take a peek at that car collection of yours?"

Jack's eyes sparkle at Alec's request. "Really?!"

Alec chuckles. "Yeah, really."

Jack shoots off the bed and sprints out of my room. Alec is laughing, enjoying his ability to bring that little boy so much happiness.

Alec slides over, filling my back with his warmness. "You sure you don't need my help in that shower?" His fingers trail over my side.

My body is tingling, begging me to give in. But that's not the proper parenting move, especially when your son doesn't even know that's his dad.

I have no idea how to even broach that with Jack. I push the thought out of my head. That is way too much to dissect right now.

With the small thread of willpower I have left, I throw the comforter off and make a beeline to the en suite, hastily shutting the door behind me. I go straight for the shower, turning the water on.

I hear Alec laughing uncontrollably.

He shouts over the noise, "Next time, I'm helping!"

It goes quiet after that. I imagine he has gone to find Jack.

"Ahh, me time," I whisper to myself. I step into the hot shower, ready to feel refreshed.

After showering, I get dressed, opting for a casual dress. It's a short-sleeved sage-green V-neck with little white flowers all over it. I quickly blow-dry my hair and run my straightener through it, deciding to skip makeup.

After cleaning up my little bathroom mess, I head out of the bathroom to find Alec and Jack. Walking through my bedroom, I'm a little shocked that my ears aren't being flooded with giggling boys.

I step into the hallway but still no sound.

What the hell?

I take a tentative step onto the stairs, shouting below, "Hello? Jack? Alec? Josh?"

Nothing.

Mom panic begins kicking in, speeding my descent off the stairs. "Jack, where are you?"

When I step off the stairs and into the living room, my eyes begin assessing everything, checking to see if anything is out of place. I scan the rest of the living room, passing over the kitchen. Then, I look down the hallway toward the front door.

My breath hitches. The door is wide open.

My feet are moving me before I realize it, taking off for the opening. "Jack! Where are—"

Two bodies jump out of the coat closet, barreling into me. Jack's shaggy brown hair catches my eye.

I'm going to kill them.

Jack bursts into laughter. "Gotcha, Mom!"

He immediately turns to Alec, eyes twinkling. Alec shuts the front door, barely containing his laughter. These boys are going to be the death of me.

My expression hasn't changed, still frozen with fear that something worse was happening.

Alec straightens up, running his hands up my arms. "Come on, Lu. It was a prank. Everything's okay."

I take a deep breath in, calming my racing heart. "I know, you jerk. It was just one you should never pull on a mom!" I smack his shoulder.

And when he smiles again, I'm unable to resist my own from taking over.

Wait, we're still missing a person.

"Where's Josh?"

Footsteps behind me grab my attention.

"Right here." He has his hand in the air. "I was told to stay in my room until you screamed." He laughs, walking up and throwing his arm over my shoulders. "You two heading out?"

A sigh leaves my lips without a thought. I love seeing my mom, but I don't love seeing her in a hospital bed.

I step out of Josh's grasp and grab my coat. "Yeah, we'd better go. I don't want to be gone too long. There's so much laundry calling my name." I bend down and kiss the top of Jack's head. "I love you, buddy. I'll be home soon."

Alec opens the door for me, gesturing for me to walk through. Once he shuts the door behind him, he wraps his hand around mine. "You ready?"

I raise my eyebrows at him. "Are you? It's a lot to take in."

His lips tilt up in a half-smile. "I'll be okay, promise."

I offer a reassuring smile. "Okay. Thanks for coming with me, Alec."

He opens the car door for me. "Of course, Lu. I do have practice at seven tonight, but I am yours every moment until then." He chuckles. "And after too." He winks.

I settle into my driver's seat, and he walks around, getting in the passenger side. The drive to the hospital is pretty quiet. I don't have anything to talk about, and he doesn't try to force conversation.

When we pull into the parking lot, it begins to rain.

Alec looks outside. "Great, even though I'm sure you're happy about it."

I smile at him, shocked he remembers. Rain has always been calming to me. I like to think that it's the universe crying, that even the universe can be so overwhelmed that it needs to let it out.

But most of all, I love the feeling of the raindrops hitting my skin. It's so refreshing, and it makes me feel at peace.

And when I step out of the car, that's exactly what I feel. And maybe exactly what I need before this.

Alec takes my hand the second he can, letting me guide him through the hospital that I now know like the back of my hand.

When we approach my mom's room, I turn to him and take a deep breath. *Here we go.*

I let him walk in first, just gauging his reaction. I look for fear or pity at all the machines hooked to her. I find neither, only sadness for the woman he once knew.

I follow him in, taking the seat I always do. I pull my chair up to the edge of the bed, wrapping her hand in mine.

"Hey, Mom. I brought a visitor today." My words catch in my throat.

She looks worse today. Her cheekbones seem to be more prominent.

"I know you remember Alec."

He rests his clasped hands on the bed next to her, focusing his attention on her face. "Hey, Mrs. Young. You raised an incredible woman, and you would be so proud of the boy she has raised." His eyes flicker down to his hands. "I'm sure you are pretty upset with me, and we have a lot to catch up on. But I'm here. I'm not going anywhere, and I plan on explaining it all to you when you wake up."

I can't remember how long it's been since I last fully cried. I know there is so much pent-up emotion inside me. If there was ever going to be a breaking moment, it would be now. But it won't break free.

Alec and I sit and talk with my mom for about an hour. He tells her all about hockey and about the first time he met Jack. She would've laughed—I know it.

I fill her in on the marketing opportunity I got. I should be starting sometime this coming week.

When we stand up to leave, I bend down and give her a kiss on the cheek.

I pat Alec's chest, ready to head out, but he steps toward her and leans in, whispering something in her ear. He kisses her forehead and then turns to me. Without a word, he takes my hand and leads me out of the room and out the way we came. With no mention of what he said. And I don't ask.

We stop at the grocery store to grab stuff for dinner. I'm going to make this garlic zucchini ramen dish I found online earlier.

When we pull into the driveway, I'm ready to get some comfy PJs on and start cooking for everyone.

Alec turns the knob on the front door, but before he can get it fully open, Josh fills the doorway with a look of terror on his face.

He runs his hands down his face, and my stomach drops.

"I'm sorry, Laura. He was asking questions that were completely natural for a little boy. Like where babies come from, how it happens, whatever. Long story short, we got done with the conversation, and he tells me he's going to go play cars upstairs." Josh's hands are waving dramatically. "Then, when he comes back down, he has a couple pictures in his hand, and … oh God, Laura, I'm sorry. I know it wasn't my place. But when he asked me, I couldn't lie to him, you know? Please don't hate me."

I grab his face in my hands. "Josh, what the hell are you talking about?"

Alec steps next to me. His voice is shaky as he demands, "Josh, spit it out!"

"He found your shoebox in the closet, the one from high school. He recognized you and Alec in the pictures. He knows, Laura. He knows."

O*h God.* All color drains from my face.

"You told him, Josh? Seriously?"

My shock is beginning to grow into anger—no, fury.

Josh steps fully out of the doorframe, pulling the door shut behind him. "Laura, I'm sorry. He straight-up asked me. He's a smart kid—you know that. And he literally had a picture of you guys from high school. It didn't take me telling him for him to figure it out."

This isn't how this was supposed to go. It was our choice to figure out how to tell him, if and when we were ready.

My anger is boiling. It needs an outlet, and it finds its target.

I grab his shirt collar and pull him down to my level. "How could you let this happen, Josh? This shouldn't have happened. It shouldn't have happened today and especially not with you. Don't you think it would have been a lot better, coming from his *actual* mom and dad?"

I slam my eyes shut, and my heart aches, knowing I've gone too far. Josh has always looked at Jack almost like a son. He watches him when I'm busy, takes him to school, and picks him up when I can't. And he always makes sure he is available for anything Jack needs.

He yanks back out of my grasp, pursing his lips. "Nice, Laura. Thanks."

Josh turns on his heels, heading back inside.

"Josh! I'm sorry!"

Josh and I will be okay. I'm just too overwhelmed right now.

Alec's hand finds my back. My eyes begin to burn. I hate confrontation, especially when I have no idea it's coming.

I knew the second those words left my mouth that I had gone too far. Josh and Charlotte are my rocks. I have no idea where I'd be today if I didn't have them in my corner.

Alec begins lightly rubbing my back. "Lu?"

Turning to him, I push back the feelings wanting to break free. "I'm okay."

He slides his hand over my cheek, cupping my jaw. I settle into the strength his simple touch gives me.

"What do you want to do?"

I know he's talking about Jack. The problem is that I have no *fucking* idea. I thought I had time. Time to figure it out, ease him into it. Not show up after visiting Mom and not having a say in how it played out.

I let out the huge sigh that's been building in my chest. "I don't know, but let's head in."

Alec furrows his brows. "Do you know what you're doing?" He offers me his hand.

I lock my fingers with his. "No fucking clue."

Alec opens the door for us, and I take the lead. I was so not prepared for this to be happening so soon. I mean, Alec and I still have a lot to talk about. We haven't made anything official yet, and he's only here on tour right now. I did not want Jack to know unless there was no doubt about us getting back together for good. I don't want his heart getting broken too.

When we walk in, the downstairs is empty. Josh is probably in his room, hating me. Charlotte's at the club, doing prep for tonight. And I imagine Jack is in his room, hoping his dream of Alec moving in will come true.

When I turn and go up the stairs, my heart is pounding. This is the exact type of moment when I need my mom. I need her to tell me what to do, how to handle this. I need her to wrap her arms around me, kiss my cheek, and tell me it will all be okay.

But she's not here to do any of that, and I've never missed her more.

Jack's door is closed, so I knock.

"Come in!" Jack shouts, seemingly far from the door, probably lying on his bed.

I take one last deep breath before opening the door. "Hey, buddy."

Jack jumps up from his bed, Legos flying onto the floor from him flinging his blanket off him. He runs over, his arms spread wide.

I bend down and embrace him in a hug, standing up with him in my arms.

He leans back, and I run my fingers through his soft hair. "We have to talk, bud, okay?"

Jack's eyes drop to the floor. "Is it about what I talked to Josh about?"

I nod. "Come on. Let's go sit downstairs."

I have a weird sense of calm, walking back down the stairs. I don't know how to explain it. I just trust that I'm here, doing my best, and I will just know what to say in the moment.

Having Jack so young was terrifying, and I have always been scared that I'm doing the wrong thing. But if I've learned anything from being a mom, it is that you will never know everything, you will never have the perfect solution, and the only thing you can do is your absolute best.

I set Jack down on the couch, sitting him to my left with Alec on my right. Jack is still avoiding my eye contact.

But then he turns to me, leans up, and whispers in my ear, "Are you mad at me, Mommy?"

I instantly cup his cheeks in my hands, locking eyes with him. "Oh, honey. No, no, no. I'm not mad at all, not at all."

"Promise?" The concern in his eyes breaks my heart.

"Yes, baby, I promise." I give him a kiss before releasing his precious little face. "Now, I know you found the old photos in my closet, and I know what you and Josh talked about. And Josh told you the truth. Alec is your dad, Jack." I rub my thumb over his tiny fingers. "I know this is probably all confusing. Your dad and I were young when I got pregnant with you. It was scary and hard because I didn't know how to be a mom. And then your dad moved away, and he never knew about you … until now."

"But why didn't you tell him?" Jack interrupts me.

"It's a long story, bud. But he's here now, and he wants to be a part of your life." I look at Alec, hoping that he feels that way.

His face says it all. His nose is flaring as he attempts to hold back the tears I can see are trying to fall.

Alec gets off the couch and kneels in front of Jack, taking his other hand. "I'm sorry, Jack. I wish I could've been here for you your whole life. I wish I could've seen you take your first steps, celebrated every birthday, watched you open your first Christmas present, dropped you off on your first day of school." His voice breaks. "I wish I'd never left your mom. I wish I'd never left you."

A lump grows in my throat at his words, making me fall for him all over again. "But you're here now."

"Does that mean I can call you Dad? I've always wanted one of those." Jack's smile is beginning to form.

Alec looks to me, his head cocked to the side in a silent plea.

How can I possibly say no after that speech?

I nod.

He turns his attention back to Jack as the first tear rolls down his cheek. "I would love that."

Jack's smile expands, looking too big for his face. I haven't seen him smile like that since before Mom was sick.

Jack stands up, placing his hands on Alec's shoulders. "Okay, Dad." He says it almost in a joking voice.

I know the two will be best friends. Jack is so much like his father that I sometimes wonder what he got from me.

Feeling a weight lift off my chest from this conversation being over, I stand up. "How about I go get dinner started, and you guys hang out here?"

Jack hops off the couch and runs to his toy bin. "Okay, Mom!"

I am heading into the kitchen when Alec whistles. I turn around, and he raises his palm to his mouth and blows me a kiss. I dramatically jump in the air, catching it and smacking it to my lips. He chuckles and then turns to Jack, and I turn around, leaving my son to play with his *dad* for the first time.

I finish making the sauce when my phone chimes. Picking it up, I see it's an email from The Crooked Spine.

> *Laura,*
>
> *We are so excited to have you start with us. Mrs. Lang has shown us some of your work, and we are thoroughly impressed.*
>
> *Next time you are in her class, fill out the paperwork. She has it.*
>
> *Have a great evening.*
>
> *Darius Corwin*
>
> *Owner of The Crooked Spine*

I can barely contain my smile as I close the email. Mrs. Lang is my hero for getting me this job. It's exactly what I want to do. I want to manage the marketing and social media of a company.

Not a lot in my life has ever gone to plan. I definitely didn't plan on getting pregnant. I didn't imagine raising my son alone. I never thought I would almost lose my mom when she had her stroke. I never expected to see Alec again.

Don't get me wrong. Jack is my light. He is the love of my life and all I will ever need.

But it definitely hasn't been easy.

I worked hard to keep bills paid and food on the table. I spent the last three years in school working as hard as I possibly could to get my education and to succeed in all my classes. And for the first time in a long time, my effort is being noticed; I'm being seen.

I lock my phone and get back to the task at hand—dinner. I strain the noodles and add them to the pan, mixing it in with the zucchini and sauce. I plate it in our sturdy black plastic bowls that I got from Target.

I call out to my boys, "Dinner's ready!"

Jack's pitter-patter gets louder, and he barrels into the kitchen, straight to the dining table. "Thanks, Mom!"

Alec walks in behind him, and I just stop. I stop thinking about all the negatives in my life, and I focus on this, taking a mental screenshot.

Alec walking into my kitchen to sit down and have dinner with our son and me is almost surreal.

It feels like after all these years, he's finally come home.

"Jack! Alec! Hurry up!" I shout.

Jack has his first official practice today. They don't do tryouts or cuts or anything. They don't want to deter kids from playing, so they just have open sign-ups. Then, you pay the registration fee and all the equipment costs.

Jack is on the Rhinos team, and their colors are gray and black. We are supposed to be at the rink in ten minutes, which is no biggie, except that the rink is fifteen minutes from the house and Jack and Alec are still upstairs in Jack's room, getting ready.

I hear Jack's pitter-patter right before he screams, "Ready!"

Alec and Jack come zooming down the stairs. Jack's eyes are dead set on the garage door, and Alec can't take his eyes off of Jack. I grab my keys off the counter and follow them out, ready to speed a little to get there on time.

The drive there is fairly quick. Every light seems to magically turn green, and we make it there with a minute to spare.

We practically run inside, trying to get to his rink.

Alec yanks the door open to the building and we find a spot in the back just before one of the coaches begins speaking.

The coach is wearing a suit and has his hands clasped behind his back. "I want to welcome all of you to the very first practice. Make sure you always have a water bottle and all your gear before walking into this rink. Without them, you will be sent home for the day."

I bump Alec's shoulder. "He knows these kids are five and six, right?"

Alec stifles a laugh. "Yes, Lu, he knows. Hockey takes a lot of dedication and time. If this is really something Jack wants to do, he is going to have to work for it. But I'm hoping he got some of his dad's skills." He winks at me before turning back to the coach.

"All right, parents, we are going to be getting fitted for skates today." He waves over a slew of people from the sidelines. "These guys are going to get your kids in the proper skates. My assistant will be running the rest of practice tonight. It will just be focusing on skating techniques. I will see you all tomorrow. Good night."

With that, he waves his hand and starts walking in our direction near exit. When he's about ten feet away, he looks up and stops walking, eyes locked on Alec.

A smile forms on his face. Hmm, I didn't know he could do that.

He approaches us with his hand extended toward Alec. "Alec Kostelecky?"

Alec takes his hand, giving a firm shake. "Yes, sir."

I swear the coach is totally fangirling over Alec right now.

"To what do I owe the honor?" he asks, completely flabbergasted.

Alec turns, smiling to me, and then lovingly looks down to Jack. "My son just joined your team." Alec slides his arm around my shoulders. "This is my girlfriend, Laura, and our son, Jack."

The coach's eyes widen as he realizes the famous Alec Kostelecky's son will be on his team.

The coach bends down to Jack's level. "Well, we are so excited to have you here, Jack." He stands back up and reaches his hand out to me. "Great to meet you, Laura." He shakes my hand and then reaches for Alec's once more before he walks off.

Jack spins around, looking at Alec, smile beaming ear to ear. "My dad's famous?"

Alec chuckles and takes Jack's hand. "Let's go get those little feet some skates."

Alec and Jack lead the way, and we get in line behind the other players and parents. When we finally reach the front of the line, I have a sense of excitement in me—for Jack, for Alec, and for myself. Our own little hockey fam.

But there is one thing I can't get out of my mind. At some point, this is going to go public, and the coach recognizing him will just be the beginning of hundreds of thousands. And I'm naive to think that the craziness of Alec's life will begin and end with him.

One of the workers waves us over. "Hey, guys, I'm Jared." He squats down to Jack and lifts his foot up, mumbling to himself. "All right, let's try these."

Jack pushes his foot down into the skate, and Jared quickly laces it up. Satisfied with the fit, he slips the other skate onto Jack's foot.

Suddenly, Jack takes off running past us in his skates. I guess Alec's genes really did get passed down.

I turn just in time to see him and Erick slam together in a hug meant for long-lost friends. Although I know for a fact that they saw each other today at school.

My chest warms when I see the two boys wrapped in each other's arms, and when they pull out of the hug, their hands stay connected.

Alec leans down to my ear. "Is-is that Jack's friend or boyfriend?" he asks genuinely.

I lean into his touch. "To be honest, I don't know, but I'm guessing boyfriend more than friend."

Alec smiles against my ear. "All righty then. I can't wait to meet him."

My mom tingles kick in, and I quickly scan the crowd, searching for the reason my hair is standing up.

And I soon spot it.

A couple is standing there, scowling at Jack and Erick. A look of pure disgust twists into the ugly death stare that is shooting toward my five-year-old, who is lost in conversation.

The couple has to be in their low- to mid-twenties. The man leans down to his wife, and as he finishes speaking what I imagine is nothing short of absolute idiocy, his eyes meet mine.

And I let my fury shine through them.

Holding nothing back in my burning gaze, I stand a little taller. One word out of his mouth, and I will become unglued.

Alec must sense my stare, and he reaches out and places a strong, supportive hand on my back.

I feel his lips brush my ear before he says, "What's going on?"

He doesn't ask if something's wrong or if I am okay. Alec knows me. He's known me almost my whole life. He doesn't have to ask if something is wrong—he just knows.

"This bigoted man is clearly not okay with Jack and Erick being, well, whatever they are. And I am currently locked in a staredown with him, waiting for him to back off."

I blink, and the next thing I see, Alec is already five feet ahead of me, walking toward the couple.

My body reacts before I realize it, stepping out toward him. I whisper, "Alec! Get back here!"

He ignores me and treks on.

I take long steps in hopes of grabbing him before he goes off on this couple. Not that they don't deserve it, but I've never been one to start a confrontation. But I'm too late.

When Alec walks up to them, a look of instant recognition sets into their features. I'm not surprised. Anyone in and around the hockey world knows who Alec is—the star center in the league right now.

The man, who five seconds ago clearly didn't approve of our son's relationship, is now stretching his hand out. "Holy shit. You're Alec Kostelecky of the Nighthawks."

Alec takes his hand and shakes it but doesn't let go. I take a step toward Alec and rest my hand on his shoulder, which is rippling with anger.

I might not be a fan of confrontation, but there's a reason Alec sees the penalty box far too often. He doesn't start fights for no reason. But the second there's any kind of threat on a person he cares about, all bets are off.

Alec's steel grip is holding the man's hand in place as he tugs him forward, bringing him inches from Alec's face. Alec towers over the man's much smaller stature.

Alec's voice is clear and calculated when he says, "Damn straight I'm Alec Kostelecky, and that right there"—Alec turns and points at our son, who's still in la-la land over there with Erick—"is my son. And I don't give a shit what your views are. But if you keep looking at my son like that, I'll get you banned from this league. One text, and you and your son are done here."

Alec pushes the man back, and he willingly goes, his face ghost white. I bet he wasn't expecting that.

The man shakes his head, and his next words are uncertain, hesitant. "I'm sorry. It won't happen again."

He grabs his wife's hand and hustles over to where his son is getting fitted for skates.

I feel on edge, and my chest is getting tight. I don't know if Alec should've threatened to get him kicked off the league. That seems like an abuse of power. Still hot, but just going a bit too far.

Alec finally turns to me, and I watch the anger in his face deplete as he takes a quick breath.

I cock my head to the side, ready to give him a little piece of my mind. But he opens his mouth and puts a finger over my lips and shushes me.

"Look, before you say whatever is brewing in that mind, hear me out. If you'd met the owner of this league and his *husband*, you would know that was not an empty threat."

Alec starts to pull his finger away, but then a twinkle shimmers in his eyes, and a smirk tugs on his lips.

He slides his finger across my cheek, cradling my head in his hand. The smirk is full-on claiming his lips as he slowly leans down. His lips graze mine, and shivers shimmy down my back.

Oh, for fuck's sake, I'm not in the mood for teasing right now.

I reach up and lock my fingers around his neck and tug him, smashing his lips into mine. He runs the tip of his tongue across the crease of my lips, and I *really* wish we weren't at the rink right now.

He's the first to pull away, and I'm so grateful he did because I think I would've had sex right here on the floor. He's addictive. Once his lips touch mine, I'm unable to stop myself.

Alec takes both my hands in his and swings them back and forth. "Don't make plans tonight." A pure look of mischief flickers in his eyes.

I furrow my brows, and my mind flashes a thousand ideas of what he could possibly have planned.

But who am I to say no to the *Alec Kostelecky?* I laugh to myself.

"Okay, but what about Jack?" I drop one of my hands out of his, and we walk over to the edge of the ice, where Jack and Erick are now skating.

He strokes his thumb across the back of my hand. "Already took care of it." He spins me toward him and takes my chin in his free hand. "Just trust me, Laura."

Now, my chest is tight for so many other reasons. But mostly, the love I have for this man, for the love that I have always had for him.

"Okay, no more questions." I turn back to the ice, but my brain instantly smacks me with a thousand questions, and I can't help but let one slip.

I turn back to him, and he already has a laugh teasing his lips.

"One question—last one, I swear. What should I wear?"

The laugh on his lips falls. "Something tight and maybe a little short." His eyes seductively drop, quickly scanning my body, causing a wave of heat to settle over my skin.

His answer only makes me want to ask a million more questions. But I keep them at bay. I now have to figure out what the hell to wear.

We walk over to Erick's parents, who welcome us with hugs and warm smiles. We end up spending the next hour or so talking with them while the boys skate around. His mom says that she is so happy that Erick has Jack, no matter what they are. Which makes any tension between us fizzle out.

At one point, Alec can't help himself and gets on the ice with them, teaching them proper form.

During the ride home, I have to physically push my lips together to stop the questions brimming on the edge of my lips. Alec tells me to be ready by nine, which means I have a little over an hour to figure out what I'm going to wear, how to do my makeup and my hair.

I should not be as nervous as I am, but dear God, it feels like the butterflies are flying so fast that they might bust through my skin.

Once we get back to the house, Jack and Alec settle into the couch, watching a movie. And I hustle upstairs and bust into Charlotte's room.

What I expected to see was Charlotte sitting on her bed. What I didn't expect? Seeing Reed and Char mid-sex.

"*Oh my God*!" I slam the door shut and cover my eyes at the same time. "Lock the fucking door!" I shout at them and book it to my room as fast as possible.

I can hear Char's giggles as I enter my room, shutting the door behind me. There are so many things I could go through life without seeing. Charlotte bent over with Reed behind her is one of them.

But I will give Charlotte a congrats because Reed is … well, he fits the hockey stereotype when it comes to dick size. But again, something I could have gone my whole life without *actually* seeing.

Trying my best to erase the burning image in my mind, I head into my closet to find something that I think will impress

Alec tonight. Although I'm sure I could show up in a cinched garbage bag, and he would be happy.

"Let's start with these," I whisper to myself as I pull five of my club work dresses off the rack and head to my mirror.

I strip out of my clothes and grab the first dress, slipping it over my head.

When I get it zipped up, Charlotte comes into the room with the biggest smile on her face. "Enjoy the show?" She laughs.

I grab one of my pillows off my bed and chuck it at her. "Shut it!" It takes me a second to realize that she's just now coming into my room. "Hold the fuck up. Did you guys finish after I came in?"

Charlotte belly-flops onto my bed. "Well, we weren't about to let you ruin the mood."

"I can't believe you." I laugh and turn to my mirror. "What do you think about this one?"

I examine the dress. Its tight deep red fabric hits right at my fingertips. It has delicate straps that crisscross in the back. It's really pretty, but I don't know if it's the one for tonight.

It would probably be a hell of a lot easier to pick a dress if I knew exactly what we were doing.

Char army-crawls across my bed to my pile of dresses. One by one, she tosses them onto the ground until only one remains.

"This one." She holds the dress up above her head.

I yank the shimmery gold fabric out of her hand and unzip the red dress in one move. I haven't worn the gold one yet, so it would still have the feeling of wearing something new.

It's probably the least modest thing I own. The front of the dress cuts into a deep V about three inches above my belly button. Two thin straps keep it on my shoulders, crossing each other on my shoulder blades, and then it drops into a very low-cut back. The length is not forgiving if I need to bend in the slightest.

He wanted tight and showy. Well, he's gonna get it.

"All right, now, help me figure out my hair." I give her a quick twirl as she stands up.

"Thank God. It needs some work." She boops my nose and drags me into the bathroom.

After forty or so minutes, we leave the bathroom, and I feel a little like a stripper—in the best way. I laugh to myself.

While I did my makeup, Char straightened my hair and pulled it up into a tight, high ponytail, wrapping a strand of my mousy-brown hair to hide the band.

I also went all out with my makeup—smoky eyes and a bright red lip.

Char heads to the bedroom door. "I'm going to put Jack in bed, so he doesn't have to see his mom dressed like a prostitute."

"Ha! Funny! An expensive *escort*, if anything." I step into my closet to find some shoes.

Opting to be a little dangerous tonight, I slip my thong off, kicking it onto the floor.

I choose a matching strappy gold heel and slip them on just as I hear the door close.

Adjusting my earring, I head out of the closet. "Wow, he must've gone down quick."

My next step is cut short. Charlotte is nowhere in sight. In her place is Alec with his jaw dropped.

His shoulders are rising and falling rapidly as he finds his words. "I think we should just skip the whole thing tonight"—he takes a step forward, and his fingers trail up my arm, fireworks bursting in his path—"and just stay right"—his burning touch grazes up my shoulder and finds the sensitive spot on the side of my neck—"here."

My eyes drift shut from his touch, and when I open them again, I swear I can see flames in his gaze.

Leaning in to my addiction to this man, I say, "O-okay."

"Tsk-tsk, *Laura*. I have way too many plans, and it would be too easy if I gave in right now. On top of that"—his fingers find their path again, and when they reach the bottom of my jaw, his thumb grabs the other side, and he takes full control of my being, squeezing the perfect amount—"if I remember right, you liked this." The pressure of his grip tightens, and I swear this dress is fighting to get off my body. "I have a few new tricks up my sleeve now. I'm not sixteen anymore, Lu. And I want to hear my damn name on those lips again."

The tightness building in my core is begging to be set free. And as his fingers release my jaw, a whimper slips past my lips. I should be embarrassed, but I'm not. I'm hoping it's enough to make him give in.

I should have known better though. That damn stubbornness of his has not changed.

I flick his chest and dart past him. "Hurry up! Let's get this over with, so we can get back here."

I don't wait for him and head downstairs, grabbing my clutch and heading out the front door. Just in time to see a stretch limo pull into the driveway. Well, this boy has way too much money on his hands. For God's sake, just get an Uber.

I can't even convince this stupid smile to get off my face. And I'm not upset in the slightest. Sometimes, I forget that the Alec I knew and the Alec I now know is not the same one that the Nighthawks fans know. I forget that he isn't just another hockey player in some league. He is *the* damn hockey player in *the* NHL.

Hearing the door close behind me, I turn to see Alec heading toward me with red roses in his hand.

He might be Alec Kostelecky, best center in the NHL, to the rest of the world. But to me, he will always be the first and only boy I've ever loved.

I take the roses from his outstretched arm. "Thank you. When did you even have time to get these?"

He waves the driver away and opens the door for me. "I can't give away my tricks, or it will ruin the magic, Lu. Duh."

I step into the limo and feel his fingers graze the back of my thigh, reigniting the fire that was burning in my bedroom. Fully getting into the limo, I sit down, and Alec finds a seat right at my side, his hand settling down on my knee.

Curiosity getting the better of me, I ask, "Are you going to tell me where we are going?"

He runs his tongue over his bottom lip, humor dancing in his smirk. "No, I don't think I will. I like watching you squirm."

I huff out a breath of defeat and place my hand under my chin. Alec's fingers begin moving on my knee, eliciting shivers on my skin.

"We're almost there," Alec says.

Soon after, the limo pulls to a stop. After a moment, the limo driver opens the door for us. And out of all the places he could've picked, I was not expecting him to pick Fireflies.

As we clamber out of the limo, I can see how packed the place is tonight. Part of me wants to clock in and help out. I imagine they are swamped inside. But I can't. I'm here for me tonight, for us.

A bright flash pulls my attention away from the entrance. A second flash goes off, and my vision finally homes in on its source.

"Over here!" someone shouts, flashes continuing to attack my eyes.

Alec's hand finds my back, and he pushes, "I'm sorry, Lu. I have no idea how they found out."

We race into the building, and I finally realize that paparazzi were the ones taking photos of us. *Actual* paparazzi.

Once we're safely inside and security blocks them from coming in, I turn to Alec. "Is that a normal occurrence for you?"

The look of seriousness washes off his face as he drags his hand across his stubbly jaw. "Yeah, unfortunately, it comes with the territory. I'm sorry, babe. They weren't supposed to ruin tonight."

My heart skips a beat when I hear him call me babe. I feel like we're sitting in Al's Barbeque.

"You just called me babe," I say, a little dumbfounded.

His brows furrow. "Is that okay?"

I take a step toward him. "Of course. It just caught me by surprise—that's all."

He takes my hand and begins pulling me toward the main room. "Good."

When the doors open, I'm stunned and a little jealous that I'm not working tonight. The place is packed! I mean, I could easily walk out of here tonight with close to a thousand dollars.

Alec leads me all the way to the bar, where Mark takes our order. I offer a small smile.

We don't talk much while we consume our first drink. We just sit at the bar, taking in the chaos on the dance floor. I get why he wanted me to wear something tight and short now.

Alec finishes his first drink and then leans down to me. "Want to know why I brought you here?"

I nod, feeling the stubble of his cheek scratch mine. That shouldn't make a wave of heat travel from my neck to my core. But here we are.

His hands find my back, and he pulls me around the stool and flush against his chest, our hips lined up indecently. "This is where we finally reunited. And I know you were here with Cam that night because he told us all about it. I almost killed him." He shrugs. "I thought it would only be fair if I got the same treatment. Before I ran into you, he texted all of us that night, saying that he had found this amazing girl who was dynamite on the dance floor. The only time you and I'd ever danced was the winter formal. And I can't imagine those were the same moves you showed him."

His hand moves from my back to my collarbone, wrapping around the base of my neck and I all but drag him to the floor to show him what he's been missing.

He laughs as we find our own spot in the mayhem. I fully open my senses, feeling the music take hold of me.

And then I let go.

Alec's hands dance on my hips, occasionally digging in, causing me to grind harder against him. We sway, the music singing in our ears and our hearts. We are free, flowing, grinding, getting lost in the high of our touch.

Finding Alec's left hand on my hip, I lace my fingers with his. Taking my right hand, I hook it up around the back of his neck, crushing us together even more.

An explosion of pleasure erupts on the crook of my neck as his tongue and lips lavish me. My fingers dig into the back of his neck, and a deep groan from his lips works its way through my body.

He bites my earlobe. "Laura, we aren't going to last all night if you keep this up."

I spin in his grip, facing him with a smirk on my lips.

Challenging him, I say, "You wanted what Cam got, right?"

Jealousy and a hint of fury erupt in his eyes. He hisses out, "Yes."

"Well then, we're just getting started." I grab his face in my hands and bring his lips to mine.

Within seconds, his lips part, and I slide my tongue between them. He moans into my mouth.

His kiss claims me, scorching my soul.

His hands begin to join in on the fun. One of his hands grabs my jaw, his fingers under one side and his thumb on the other. And then I lose control—Alec takes it all.

He tightens his grip, and pulsing aches throb between my legs. Tilting my head, he runs his lips and teeth down my jaw, latching on to that sweet spot on my collarbone.

A gasp slips past my lips, and honestly, I couldn't care less that we're in the middle of the dance floor right now. I want him. I *need* him.

"Alec," I whimper.

"What?" His voice is animalistic when he comes up for air.

"Let's go," I beg him. I don't know how much longer I can wait before spontaneously combusting.

He hesitates. I can see he's fighting it. He probably had a whole night of plans that I am totally vetoing.

"Please." I graze my finger on the edge of his pants, slipping in into his waistband.

His eyes flutter closed, and his lips part. "Fuck."

Without another word, he is practically running towards the exist with my hand in his. He shoots a quick message on his phone, and when we get outside, the limo is pulling up.

A lec doesn't wait for the driver. He is already opening the door, ushering me inside, past the flashing lights.

The driver has the partition down. "Sir?"

"Take us to 115 Harlow Drive," he announces. "And put the partition up."

I gulp.

"Wait, what? That's not my address." I turn to him.

He just smiles and fishes something out of his pocket—a hotel key. "I know. I got us a suite for the night. And don't worry; Charlotte already knows. Enough talking. Come here."

And with that, his tongue finds mine once again. His hands grab my waist, and in one swift movement, he pulls me onto his lap, my hips straddling him.

I sink into the position and am shocked to feel the already-hard bulge beneath me. His hands race to my hips and bunch the fabric up, completely exposing me.

His hands explore, and when they trail closer to my center, Alec pulls back. "You're not wearing any underwear."

I bite my lip, unable to even find words from the blood pounding in my ears.

He takes a deep breath before saying, "I love you, Laura. I always have. You're the only woman I've ever loved and the only one I ever will."

He keeps his gaze locked on to mine as his fingers find my center and begin making small circles.

My eyes begin to drift shut, but he grabs my chin with his other hand and demands, "Look at me."

I force my eyes open, and my head kicks back as a finger slips into my entrance. My eyes flutter shut again but he wiggles my chin, shaking my eyes open. After a few pumps, a second finger joins in the torturous rhythm. His thumb finds the pulsing bundle of nerves, and with the smallest pressure, whimpers begin falling from my lips.

Alec's free hand finds the back of my neck, and he holds me up. Desire and raw, unbridled need burn in his eyes.

His pace quickens, and I can feel my core tightening, ready to release.

"Alec," I moan. "Please."

The limo pulls to a stop, and I've never been more annoyed and frustrated in my life.

"Soon," Alec says as he leans in and kisses my forehead.

I hear footsteps outside, and I throw myself off of Alec's lap and adjust my dress just as the door opens.

"Mr. Kostelecky," the driver says.

Alec leads the way, and I follow closely behind. When I step outside, I realize we're at the Sheraton Hotel. I've driven by this place a thousand times.

The driver shuts the door and offers his hand to Alec. "Text me in the morning, and I will be here."

"Thanks, Tom," Alec replies, shaking his hand.

The driver nods and heads back to his side.

Alec locks his hand with mine and leads us into the hotel. We bypass the desk and head straight for the elevator.

No words are exchanged as we ride up to the sixth floor. The ding of the elevator sounds worlds away. We step onto the floor, and Alec slides the key into the door closest to us.

It opens, and my heart is in my throat. As ready as I was to sleep with him in the limo, I'm nervous. This is real. We're together, against all odds.

But I have to push my fears and insecurities aside. Because despite those odds, here we are. And I don't want to waste a second.

I set my clutch on the table and turn to Alec, who's already on the edge of the bed, unbuttoning his shirt. When his eyes find mine, any lingering fears dissipate. This is right where I am supposed to be.

I float over to the bed and stand between his legs. With one hand, I guide his chin up to look at me.

My breath catches. No uncontrolled desire lingers in his gaze, but raw love and hope sit in its place.

I throw my knees over his lap, straddling him. I open my mouth to speak, but he stops me. Again.

"Before you say anything, before we do anything else, I need you to know this." He takes my cheeks in his hands. "Laura, I love you. I've always loved you. I never should have let you slip away in the first place. And I don't care if you've been with a thousand guys since me. I don't care if you slept with half my team."

I laugh at his hypotheticals.

"But I am never walking away from you or Jack again. And I will spend the rest of our lives making up for the time I missed. You are my—" He cuts off, searching for the right words as his eyes well up, before continuing, "*Everything*. I've loved you since I was sixteen, and I'm never going to stop. A hole has been in my chest, a feeling of despair. I didn't know it until I saw you at Fireflies. But the second I did, it was like I came back to life and that hole was filled again."

My breaths are huffing in and out. And it isn't until his thumb sweeps my cheek that I realize I'm crying. I've been waiting for what feels like forever to hear him say that.

I don't have anything to say. He used up all the words. So, instead, I kiss him.

I kiss his lips, but it's so much more than that. I give myself over to him, heart and soul. Although he might have had them this whole time.

He deepens the kiss, his tongue parting my lips. My hips involuntarily begin rocking against him, causing soft groans to pour into my mouth.

Alec's rough, callous hands delicately sweep across my back, slowly guiding the zipper down. The straps fall off my shoulders, and I stand, the dress pooling at my feet.

Alec bites his lip and pulls his arms out of his shirt, tossing it next to my dress.

Holy shit ...

Every inch of his torso and shoulders is defined, and I want to explore it all with my tongue.

He rises off the bed and undoes the belt of his pants, shimmying out of them.

He reaches for the band of his boxers, but I stop him, placing my hands over his. I slide my fingers into the band and gently pull them down, his large erection bouncing from the release.

Alec's hands find their home on my jaw, and I relinquish the control I had.

"Come here," he orders as he guides my mouth back to his.

His tongue dances with mine. He spins us around and places one hand around my back. With impressive strength, he lowers us down to the bed, bearing his weight on the hand by my head, our lips never separating.

When he pulls his hand out from behind my back, his fingers find that tortuous rhythm on my center. A second later, two fingers begin pumping in and out, and my eyes roll from the overwhelming sensations.

Alec's forehead falls onto mine, his lips pulling away for the first time since we found the bed. "You're so beautiful, Lu." His fingers stop their rhythm, and my body instantly misses it. "Are you ready? You're okay?"

His eyes find mine, and they are so vulnerable, so genuine, that a lump forms in my throat.

I nod my head.

He chuckles. "I need to hear you say it, Laura."

He rolls a condom on and delicately lines himself up with me, his tip slightly pressing into my entrance.

My fingers dig into the sheets with anticipation. "Yes, yes, please yes."

The largest smile graces his lips as he slowly fills me, inch by inch. I can feel him stretching me, feel him hitting spots deep inside that I didn't know existed.

My head rolls back, my mouth falling open.

Alec moans, "Laura, look at me. Don't stop."

Lifting my head up, I find his stare.

"Can we make a deal?" His voice is husky.

I can feel his control slipping.

At this point, he could tell me he was going to kill me tonight, and I'd be like, *Sounds good, babe.*

"Anything," I whisper to him.

The most devilish smirk appears. "Next time, I will take my time with you, kiss every inch of your body." He slows his thrust down, moving torturously slow. "But right now, I want to be rough with you, and *fuck* you hard, until you come screaming my name."

I've *never* been more turned on in my life. "Okay. Then, fuck me."

And holy shit, he does exactly that.

In one swift move, he grabs my legs, lifting them up and setting them on his shoulders. And if I thought he was filling me before, I was so wrong.

With every thrust, he finds new nerves, pulling moans and whimpers out of my mouth.

With my legs hooked over his shoulders, he picks up speed, thrusting faster and faster. I can feel the tingles in the bas of my spine coming, and I have never been more ready to plummet off the edge into pure fucking heaven.

He pulls out so far that I can feel the tip slip out. Then, he plunges back into me, finding that quick pace again. It's so intense.

His name drags out of my mouth as my legs quiver, "Alec," my voice is laced with need.

"Open your eyes. I want you watching me as you come." he commands.

My eyes fly open. Beads of sweat run down his chest, and the way he's looking at me, like watching me come undone by him is all he ever wants to see, is the final push.

"Come for me." he demands.

And my body obeys.

The release rips through me, shaking my legs. The pleasure hits me over and over in waves. And with one last thrust, Alec joins me in our perfect bliss.

When we walk into the arena, my senses are overwhelmed. The noise of the building crowd is already so loud. Teal and black floods my vision. This is definitely a Nighthawks game.

Every season, they change their jersey colors to represent a certain cause. This year they chose teal for ovarian cancer. One of Alec's teammates wife passed away last year from ovarian cancer and they didn't hesitate to choose teal for the season. A percentage of all the tickets sold goes towards cancer research this season.

Next season, they will choose a new cause and their jerseys will don a new color.

I begin looking around, seeking the face of the man I love.

And soon enough, I find him, lost in a crowd, signing autographs. The sight is strange for so many reasons. He will never be the famous hockey star in my mind, only the scrawny sixteen-year-old who taught me how to skate.

When he looks up and locks eyes with me, he quickly finishes his signature and walks straight to me.

Alec in sweatpants is sexy, but nothing could have prepared me for seeing him in his full gear with his helmet in his hand as he walks over to me in his skates.

The Nighthawks logo on his chest is just below my eye-level as he reaches me, picking me up like I weigh nothing. I wrap my legs around his waist, and he wastes no time in showing me just how much he missed me with kisses.

A couple flashes go off, and I pull away from Alec, knowing our affection needs to end before it goes too far, which it inevitably would.

Alec lowers me to the ground and places a wet kiss on my forehead. "I know I have to get on a flight after this, but I promise I'll be back at some point next week."

Feeling a lump form in my throat, knowing that this is the last time I'll see him before he leaves, I nod my head. "I know. We'll be okay. Next week will be here before we know it."

Alec smiles and then turns his attention to Jack, bending down to his level. "Next week, we will get on the ice and get you started on some real training. I love you, Jack."

Jack lunges, throwing his arms around Alec's neck. "I love you too, Dad."

Alec's eyes water as he stands up, his knuckles whitening on his helmet. "See you guys soon. Wish me luck."

I smile. "You've never needed luck."

Alec walks off, immediately being harassed by the paparazzi and fans, and I look down to Jack. His face is in awe as he watches his dad. And I can't help but laugh at Jack's team spirit. Cameras flash our way, and I pray that wherever those photos end up, I look relatively presentable. I laugh to myself.

Jack smiles, creasing the paint. He wanted to paint his face, so Char went all out. She admires her work as Josh, Char, Jack and I make our way to our seats. Teal and black face paint, custom Kostelecky jersey, teal-and-black-sprayed hair—the works. Jack was practically squealing when we were getting him ready. I shot a text to Alec with a pic of Jack wearing a jersey with his name on it. He quickly replied.

Perfection. See you after the game. I love you.

Right as we get settled into our seats, the light show begins, and the booming announcer begins listing off the Minnesota Mystics starting lineup.

"This is crazy though, right?" Char shouts to me over the roaring music. "I feel like we were just watching him in his Greyhounds jersey. Now, every person in this place is wearing his last name on their back."

I quickly scan the crowd around us and am a little shocked to see that hundreds of people are wearing Alec's jersey, the number sixteen showing on the shoulder of their jerseys.

"It's *insane*," I say back to her, shell-shocked.

She leans into me, whispering, "And that right there is all yours. None of these puck bunnies will ever get what you have."

I smile to myself. Huh, I really did steal America's bachelor.

Deep bass rattles the crowd as the announcer screams, "Are you ready for your Nighthawks starters?!"

The crowd erupts with cheers and chants.

"Here's your goalie—number 33, Matt MacArthur! At wing, number 72, Brett Burnssss!" the announcer shouts. "Your wing, number 19, Cam Cossssstello!"

The girls beside us scream as Cam barrels onto the ice, pumping his stick in the air.

"Number 42, defenseman, Reed Larinskiiiii!" Char goes crazy next to me, shouting and screaming for Reed. "Number 66, defenseman, Jensen Donnelleyyyy!" He drags parts of their names out, adding to the intensity of the already-electric crowd.

"It's time to put your hands together for the one, the only, the best center in the NHL, the captain of our New York Nighthawks—number 16, Aleeeec Kosteleckyyyyyy!"

The crowd explodes. Hands are flailing; feet are stomping. I slap my hands onto Jack's ears as he watches his dad shoot onto the ice, stick high in the air. Vibrations rumble through my feet from the intense noise in the arena.

Charlotte and Josh are cheering along with the crowd.

We made up pretty quickly after I yelled at him when I found out he told Jack that Alec is Jack's dad. We've always been so close that we sat down, got our thoughts and emotions out, hugged it out, and moved on. I did also buy him his favorite dove chocolates to help smooth things over too.

Jack pushes my hands away and screams, *"Go, Dad!"*

My chest warms. *Look where we are right now. Look at how far we have come.* A wave of prickles assaults the backs of my eyes. I wish my mom was here with us, she would love to see Alec play. She was always one of his biggest supporters.

Alec skates over to where we are seated, places his glove against the glass, and blows me a kiss. I air-catch it and try to ignore the gasps and oohs exploding around us. As well as the glares and scoffs.

But I can't ignore the announcer when he says, "Looks like Kostelecky has someone special here. Better get at least two goals for her tonight, Number 16."

My face burns from the attention.

Charlotte nudges me. "Even I'm a little jealous of you."

I scoff at her, "You're literally dating Reed!"

She laughs lightheartedly. "Yeah, but every girl in here wants to be you. And my ego could use a little of that right now."

"Charlotte, if your ego gets any bigger, you'll explode." I nudge her back.

After the national anthem, the lights above the ice turn on, illuminating the arena and all the players. Being up against the glass is intense, and the players look huge. Well, I mean, they are huge, but still.

Alec and the center of the other team—number 22, Rit Hamonson—head to the ref, who's waiting for the puck drop.

Alec and Hamonson lower their sticks slightly in anticipation. The ref blows the whistle, and the puck slaps the ice. Alec's and Hamonson's sticks attack the puck, fighting to get possession.

Alec manages to kick it out to Cam, and they take off. The puck slides into the zone not a second before our boys do.

Jack cheers and throws his hands into the air. Suddenly, he falls forward, crashing into the hard plastic back of the seat in front of him.

His cry pierces my heart, and I drop to the cold concrete, scooping him up into my chest as he cries.

"Shh, baby, it'll be okay," I tell him, rocking him back and forth.

Jack's cries wither away.

I glance up, instinctively looking to find Alec on the ice.

It's mid-play. Cam passes it to Reed, who weaves between two Mystics forwards. Reed glides into the right wing, Alec close behind him. Reed digs into the ice, winds his stick up, and swings. But no puck goes flying. On the swing back, Reed passes the puck right to Alec.

And Alec *misses* it.

Because Alec isn't watching Reed or the puck. He's standing straight up, looking right at me. His eyes seem to be locked on to mine. And I can see the worry in how he's standing—alert, straight up with his chest huffing in and out as he watches Jack in my arms.

The man in a suit on the Nighthawks bench shouts at Alec, "What in the fuck was that?! KOSTELECKY!"

Coach immediately turns, trying to find what has his captain so distracted.

When his gaze passes over me, it continues on to the next person only for a second. Then, it darts back to me. His eyes narrow, and his lips curl.

Another player pulls his attention back to him, and the game continues.

The next few possessions have no effect on the score. And the remainder of the first period is just as eventful. The crowd boos Alec as the Nighthawks head to the locker room.

Jack turns to me with the biggest smile I've ever seen. "I want to be on the ice one day in the NHL, just like dad."

It's amazing how oblivious young children can be to their surroundings sometimes. Maybe not exactly like Alec right now. He's probably just warming up. Although the anxiety creeping into my chest is wondering if his head is off right now, maybe being here is too much of a distraction for him.

"I think you can do anything, but it's going to take years of work, Jack," I say to him, running my fingers through his somehow already-messy hair.

He gives me that know-it-all look. "I know, Mom."

Char bumps my shoulder with her own. "Want to grab a bite?"

My stomach grumbles, as if on cue.

I nod back to her and lean to see Josh. "You want anything? I'm going to leave Jack here."

He just smiles at me. "I'm good, thanks!"

"All right, we'll be right back," I shout to him over the noise.

Charlotte and I make our way to the concessions and join the never-ending line. It moves surprisingly fast, and before we know it, we are already in our seats, and the second period is beginning.

The start is slow, no goals on either end. With minutes remaining in the period, one of the Mystics players gets a two-minute penalty for boarding Reed. Charlotte almost loses it. And Alec skates right up to the offender who checked Reed.

The smile stretched on Alec's face is all menace. I know who just became his target. The refs skate over the second Alec approaches.

It quickly fizzles out, although I'm not so sure the tension between Alec and the Mystics player did.

And with ten seconds left, Hamonson sneaks a goal right past Matt.

We leave the second period down by one.

The intermission seems to fly by. Jack and I go up to the merch shop and each pick up a Kostelecky hoodie and four foam fingers.

When we get back to our seats, I chuck one of the foam fingers at Char and then Josh. They giggle and shove their hands into their fingers, proudly waving them in the air. And the third period is underway.

The tension on the ice is palpable. The score remains tied through the first fifteen minutes. Hamonson is thrown in the penalty box for two minutes for high-sticking.

The announcer's voice blares through the speakers. "The Nighthawks are on a power plaaaay!"

Cam gains possession of the puck, passing it off to Jensen, who slides it over to Brett Burns. Brett dishes it to Alec. Only one player stands between Alec and the goalie. Alec throws it back to Cam and then slaps his stick on the ice.

The quick movement draws the player away from Alec. Cam throws it back to Alec. And as the puck glides toward him, he winds up and shoots.

And *misses*.

"Kostelecky misses again! We've never seen this from him. What is going on tonight?!" the announcer screams into the mic.

The Mystics take off with the puck. They barrel toward our goal. The winger's shot bounces off the pole. Matt dives out of the crease, aiming to grab the puck.

Number 48 on the Mystics digs into the ice and takes off for Matt. A sonic boom erupts in the air as number 48 attacks Matt, checking him back into the net. Matt bounces off the pole with a deafening thud.

The crowd falls silent.

Except for our boys.

All five of them take off after number 48.

But the other team dives in, each matching with a Nighthawk.

And Alec makes his choice—number 48.

Alec flicks his wrists, his gloves shooting down and onto the ice. Number 48 reciprocates. And fists fly. Alec lands blow after blow, and blood marks the ice. The second number 48 hits the ground, the refs interfere, pulling Alec off of him. It takes two of the three refs.

The rest of the boys are still lost in their fights. Once Alec is off the guy and escorted to the bench, the refs break up the fights one by one.

Eventually, all the fights are broken up, and the refs kick all twelve boys out of the game.

Matt is able to get up, but he looks very confused and dazed. Coaches and trainers guide him off the ice.

The crowd cheers and chants for Matt, and it continues as the final face-off puck is dropped.

And the Nighthawks *lose* the game.

Because of Alec.

Because of Jack and me. We pulled his attention during the first shot, and I don't think it's too far of a leap to know that we are why his head was so out of the game tonight.

The aftermath of the game is just as energetic as the pregame, if not more. Except everyone is booing the Nighthawks and talking about how Alec was the reason they lost tonight. We hastily make our way out of the seating area and are heading out of the arena when I hear my name being called.

I turn, confused. And my heart plummets to my stomach, and chills sweep my arms when the head coach approaches me.

I swivel, checking for Jack. But I see his hand locked in Charlotte's, and they're already heading out of the door.

"Can I speak with you for a second?" The coach's tone is as cold as the rink.

"Of course."

What am I going to do, say no to Alec's coach? Nope.

"Did you enjoy the game?" he asks me.

My mind races, and my words come out a little too fast. "It could have been better, but I'm sure everyone did their best."

"Yes, except their best was not enough tonight. And our star player cost us this game. Do you know how embarrassing it is to lose a game to one of the worst teams in the league when you are the best? All because Alec was distracted with *you*. I'm guessing his absences from practice lately were also because of *you*." His voice is short and sharp.

And anxiety begins threading into my chest with each heartbeat.

Absences from practice? Alec didn't mention anything. I just assumed he'd been hanging out with us in his free time.

Without waiting for my response, he offers me a smile, but it is the furthest thing from friendly. "I am going to tell you this once, so listen. If you refuse to follow my instructions, you will solely be responsible for the absolute destruction of Alec Kostelecky's career. Am I understood?"

I shake my head. "I'm sorry, what?"

There's no way the words I heard could've come from his mouth.

He takes a step closer to me. "I was clear. Alec has missed practices because of you. And he lost this entire game because he was concerned for the little boy and for you. His head and focus are clouded. If you do not leave him alone, I will make damn sure that he never sets foot on the ice for the rest of his contract here. Or any contract after for that matter."

Dumbfounded, I ask, "You're serious?"

He takes a step back and straightens his tie.

He looks around, smiles, and waves to fans while he says, "You have twenty-four hours, or he's done."

And with that, he turns, leaving me with my heart in pieces on the floor.

I should tell him to shove it, to fuck off, that his opinion would never and could never affect my life. I should run to Alec, I should tell him the threat that his coach made.

But am I willing to be the reason that his entire life's work is thrown in the trash?

I would like to think that Alec would be calm and smart with handling this, but Alec is a man driven by his emotions. He would probably beat the seat out of the coach and for sure get thrown off the team, and with the sway his coach has in the league, he would be done.

I will find a way around this, I just need some time. I need some time to figure out how to go around him, how to keep our family together and to keep Alec on the team. But I just don't know how to do that quite yet.

As my lip starts to tremble, the world around me seems to slow.

When did it get so quiet in here?

My body takes control, my mind is numb. My legs carry me outside, through the never-ending people and cars.

My hand opens the passenger door of the car, where Charlotte, Josh, and Jack are waiting.

I can't hear their words as I slide into the seat. My hand grabs ahold of the buckle and latches me into place.

My shoulders move, and water runs down my face.

Not moving.

Shaking, rapidly rising and falling.

Not water.

My fingertips touch my cheeks—tears.

There's only one voice that breaks through the silence. "Mommy, why are you crying?"

As if my ears were hearing for the first time, sound floods in. Charlotte's and Josh's voices blend with the medley of horns honking, cars starting, and cheering that has spilled into the parking lot of the arena.

I nod my head. "I'm okay, buddy. I'll be okay."

"Laura, what happened?" Charlotte's voice is scared, a hollow whisper.

"Later, please." I nod to Jack, who is looking out the window.

"Of course. I love you, Lu. Whatever it is, it will be okay." She squeezes my shoulder and leans back against the backseat, next to Jack.

Josh offers me a sad smile as he pulls out of the parking lot, farther and farther away from Alec.

Leaning my head against the window, I can't get three words out of my mind—*twenty-four hours*.

Even if it's only until I find a solution, I still only have twenty-four hours to break up with Alec. I wish I could let him in on my plan, but as much as I love Alec, that temper of his would get the best of him.

I have to walk away for now, for a short while, but not for long, I won't be able to stay away. Just long enough until I can take his stupid coach down.

He has spent his entire life to get to where he is. It would be selfish of me to stay with him right now. How could I say that I loved him if I was the reason he lost the most important thing in his life?

We just found each other again, and now, we have to say good-bye, even for just a moment. It's not fair.

But if I've ever learned anything in life, it's that nothing is fair, and you just have to fucking deal with it.

I don't know how I am going to tell Jack. I'll need to come up with a good lie, maybe that Alec just can't come back for a while right now. I don't know, I'll come up with something. And I know for a fact that I can't tell Charlotte what's really going on because she will run right to Reed to try to fix it. So, let's add another lie to the mix.

And then another and another, and soon, everything out of my mouth will be a made-up story that I can't unravel.

I am lost in my own mind.

The ride home happens in a flash. And Jack is asleep by the time we pull into the driveway.

I'm about to ask Char if she can take Jack in, but when I turn to her, her eyes bulge so big that I lose the words.

"Oh, Laura." Her tone is full of sorrow.

My fingers dance across my face, feeling for whatever caught her eye.

I don't feel anything there. I think Char might just be crazy until my fingers touch my eyes.

The puffiness proves her sanity.

"Oh," I whisper.

Char's eyes drift over to Jack. "Head inside, love. I got it."

With all my remaining energy, I nod and stumble out of the car.

Josh is helping Jack out of the car, lifting him into his arms to carry into the house.

My steps are heavy as I drag myself to the front door. Silence attacks my ears, begging to be broken up with the laughter of Alec and Jack.

But that's not going to happen.

My sadness carries me upstairs. I crave the softness of my bed.

Where Alec and I slept together after years spent apart.

At some point while I was lost in my thoughts in the car, I decided to handle this breakup in the quickest way I could think of—one phone call. I have to think of it as a breakup, because if I don't I'll slip up and say that it's just until I can find a way around his dumb ass coaches order.

I pull his contact info up.

And as my feet pad the carpet of my bedroom, I hit the Call button to call the love of my life and to destroy the happiness we both found again.

But his pain will be temporary, and soon, we will be back together. But for right now, this is only temporary to me, to him, it's forever. And I hope he can forgive me. But that time is not now.

It rings once, twice.

My heart jumps to my throat as I anticipate his smooth, deep voice greeting me like nothing is wrong.

On the third ring, he picks up. "Hey, Lu. Make it home okay? I miss you already."

My voice drifts through my lips, the lies flowing scarily easily. "Yeah, we're home. Your flight leaves soon?"

"Yeah, about to board in a minute." He hesitates. "Are you okay? You sound kind of off." His concern shines through.

The lies continue without effort. "Yeah. But, Alec, I—we need to talk."

Silence rings in my ears, and then his voice goes quiet. "Is everything okay?"

My phone vibrates in my hand, but I ignore it.

My chest burns, and I grab the edge of the Band-Aid and rip. "No. Alec, I—as much as I thought this was working, that I was happy, I'm not. And I- we can't do this anymore, okay? We-we can't pretend that after all this time, everything will be fine. This isn't working for me, and I'm not happy anymore." My voice breaks. "The long distance won't work, the paparazzi, everything is just too much."

His tone shifts as he says in utter disbelief, "You're serious? You can't be serious, Laura. What is going on?"

My hand slams to my open mouth to stop the soul-shattering cries from breaking free.

"Laura, I'm about to run out of this fucking airport. Fuck this jersey. Fuck this contract. I will break it right now. But I can't lose you, Laura. I can't fucking lose you again."

There's a shout in the back, but I can't make it out.

"I'm coming. Stay right where you are. I'm coming to you."

I manage to push two words through my trembling lips. "Alec, please."

His words crack when he speaks, and I can practically see the tears in his gorgeous eyes. "Laura, please don't do this. Please. I love you. I've loved you since I was sixteen years old, and I'll love you when we're fifty, eighty, a hundred. For God's sake, Laura, it's only ever been you. Since the day I first met you, your name has been branded on my soul. I can't lose you, Laura. I can't lose Jack. I didn't know I was ready to be a dad, but Jack … he-he's my son, and the second I met him, I never wanted to be anything more than his dad. More than I ever wanted this jersey."

There's a beat of silence, and then he quickly takes a large breath in. "Lu, p-please don't."

The last string holding my heart together is cut with my next words. "I don't want to be with you anymore, Alec. It was fun to relive old memories. But that's all it was—a walk down memory lane. I'm sorry, Alec. I'm sorry. We can finish out details with Jack later. I need some time to myself. Get on the plane. Don't come here. I promise you it won't change my mind. Good-bye, Alec."

The air is heavy with silence, with all the broken promises that are tearing through me, and I imagine him too right now. He's quiet, and I wish I could read his mind. But it's probably for the best that I can't.

I end the call, and a bomb goes off in my chest, a black hole forming in its place. I know that for me this break won't last forever. But I just broke his fucking heart, and I can't stop the pain of that from slicing my chest. The black hole sucks everything in. It takes all remaining happiness from my body.

I check my phone for the missed call. It's just the hospital. Probably calling about the bills, like they always do.

Sometime during the call with Alec, I ended up in my bed. I grab the edge of my covers and yank them up and over my head.

Sobs break through my chest, stabbing pains throbbing with each breath.

I hear a knock on my door, and after the next gasp of air, I hear the door open.

Soft steps grow louder, and then two arms wrap themselves around me.

"Let it out, Lu. I'm here." Char's hands rub up and down my arms.

I curl into her, trying to permanently seal our bodies together so that I never again have to be alone.

My body shakes.

Char holds me for what feels like hours. Eventually, sleep creeps into my peripheral vision. But I'm terrified to dream. Because they will all be of Alec.

And in the split second in the morning when I wake, I won't remember this. When it hits, it's going to feel like a train, demolishing my heart and soul all over again. But then, I will be angry at the coach, furious for his attempt to tear us apart. And I will do everything in my power to fix it.

M om sighs. "If you need anything at all, call me."

"Mom, I'll be fine. Trust me."

She's always been overprotective of me. Probably because it's only her and me.

Giving her a reassuring smile, I hop out of the car and shut the door behind me, and then I walk up to the school doors.

I immediately scan the crowds of people, looking for Charlotte, my best friend.

There.

I bolt up the stairs and reach for the door handle, but before I grab it, it slams open, knocking me backward off the top of the stairs.

My hair rushes forward from my fall, and I brace for impact.

But the pain never comes. Strong arms catch me, one arm under mine and the other under my knees. My body freezes midair.

I exhale sharply at the impact. And when I glance up, embarrassment hits me all over again.

The most gorgeous golden-hazel eyes peer down at me, and luscious, full lips open and laugh. And holy shit, Alec Kostelecky is carrying me right now.

"Are you okay?" He smiles, and my stomach flutters.

Everyone knows who Alec is, our town's shining hockey star, destined for the NHL. He is all every girl talks about.

And right now, he is holding me in his arms.

I nod my head, maybe a little too violently. "Yes. Thank you."

He smiles again, which damn near gives me a heart attack. He adjusts me in his arms before saying, "I'm Alec. And you are?"

Instead of saying my name, I say the first word that comes to mind, "Clumsy."

My cheeks redden even more.

His smile fills out, revealing the cutest dimple in his left cheek. "Just Clumsy? No last name?"

His finger twitches, and it dawns on me that he is still holding me in his arms in front of our school. I wiggle a bit to signal him to put me down, but he doesn't let go. Instead, he tightens his grip.

"You can put me down, you know?" I glance to the ground, my heart hammering in my chest.

He laughs, and I feel it reverberate through his body and into mine. "I know. Maybe I just don't want to yet."

My chest tingles with his words. "You don't even know me. Yet you're just going to stand here and hold me?" I laugh.

Before I know it, he's moving, heading to the double-door entrance to our school. Someone opens the door for us, and Alec walks right through it with me in his arms.

Everyone stares at us as we pass them, every single girl and almost every guy.

Alec finally speaks when we walk into the main hallway by the office. "Where's your first class?"

I all but laugh in his face, but then his hazel eyes glance down to my blue ones, and laughing is the furthest thought from my mind. "English 101 with Effertz. Room 110."

His dimple makes an appearance again as he picks up his pace and turns down a new hallway. "I happen to know just where that is. Because it's my first class too."

What in the hell is happening?

Alec slows to a stop and just stands there, looking into my eyes. His fingers loosen their hold as he lowers me to the ground. "This is our stop."

I avoid meeting the eyes of the students who I'm sure are all looking our way. Alec gestures for me to walk past him into the room. I step forward and am a little shocked when I see the desks. In place of the traditional desks are tables that sit two.

I veer left and stop at the first table, expecting Alec to find a seat at the back of the class. But when I pull one of the chairs out, Alec pulls out the other.

Oh, this is not going to end well.

When I settle into my seat, Alec leans over—too close— making goose bumps spread their way from my ear down my neck. "So, Clumsy, what's your real name?"

I stick my hand out, and when he takes it, I swear I feel a shock.

"I'm Laura. Laura Young."

Waking up this morning feels like I am digging myself out of a grave. It takes me two hours to get ready. I have to redo my makeup about three times because I keep breaking down halfway through. I miss Alec. When I woke up, I checked my phone, but not a single call or text. But Alec has always been respectful, whether it was to be held for hours, or given some space, he was always there for me however I needed him to be.

Grabbing my powder-blue pantsuit, I get dressed in a haze. With one last look in the mirror, I grab my purse with my marketing plan for The Crooked Spine and head out the door.

Charlotte doesn't work at Fireflies until tonight, so she volunteered to watch Jack while I'm gone. I need to visit my mom today too.

I saw a voice mail from the missed call last night. I ignored it because I'm sure it's a verbatim message of the other messages they've left in the past.

The Crooked Spine is only about four blocks from the house, so at least I don't have too much time to get trapped in my thoughts while I drive.

Walking up to the beautiful brick building, I pause before heading inside. This could be the start of a change for the better for Jack and me. And I can't let what's going on with Alec ruin that.

Taking a deep breath, I do my best to leave all my pain and heartache at the door.

I'm immediately greeted by one of the workers. She offers a polite smile. "Hey, how can I help you?"

I smile back. "I'm here for a meeting with Mr. Corwin."

Her arm gestures to the back of the shop. "Mr. Corwin is waiting for you in our main conference room, right past our YA section."

The Crooked Spine also hosts other business meetings. Their conference rooms are always available to be rented out.

"Thank you," I reply and walk straight ahead with a little bit of hope sneaking back into my body.

The door is open, and I walk in. Darius is sitting at the table along with a woman I don't recognize.

He rises when he sees me. "Laura, just the woman I wanted to see."

My customer-service persona kicks in. "Well, I sure hope so! Been working my butt off for you."

He laughs and gestures to the seat across from them. "Well then, let's get started. Oh, this is Alyssa, the store manager of sales of this location. We want to test out your plans here, and then depending on the results, we would like to push it into all stores by the end of the year."

Holy shit.

No one ever said anything about going nationwide with *my* work.

I take a seat, my hands shaking a little, and start setting out my plans.

Once I feel organized and comfortable, I begin to tell him everything I've come up with.

I walk them through my marketing campaign. Starting next month, we should set TikTok-trending tables in every store. I also tell them this might be productive with any other socials that are blowing up as well.

Then, I share my ideas about working with indie authors and how this is a group of authors with immense followers and readers, who are often skipped over in corporate stores.

I suggest setting up a schedule with author signings and spotlighting an indie author every month.

By the time I finish my presentation, I have the biggest smile on my face. And both Darius and Alyssa give me a standing ovation, which feels a little silly, as they're the only people in the room.

The high of the presentation quickly fades as I walk outside. The reality of Alec being gone crashes through me again.

I thought I could handle hurting him for a short while, but I wasn't ready for it to crush my soul.

I fumble with my keys as I unlock my door, my vision blurring from the tears welling.

I don't think I can do this. I think I have to tell Alec. I need to call him, to hear his voice, to soothe the burn in my chest.

I reach for my phone and scroll through my Contacts to his number and hover over the Call button.

My heart is begging me to press it, but I'm afraid that my heart might lose this battle. I can't be selfish enough to take his entire life's work away from him even if he might be selfless enough to lose it all for us.

I lock my phone and chuck it behind me, hearing it smack the backseat.

If I can't have Alec right now, I will go to my next best listener—my mom. I would give anything to hear her voice right now.

The last time I met with the doctors, they said that with each day, it's less likely that she'll wake up. But I refuse to accept the fact that she'll be gone one day.

My mom is my best friend, and she's the only one I want to talk to right now.

"Laura! Get in here!" my mom hollered from the kitchen.

I rolled my eyes and dragged myself and my swollen ankles over the worn carpet. And when I turned the corner to the kitchen, tears stung the backs of my eyes.

She had her arms gesturing to the counter filled with all sorts of stuff for Jack—a car seat, bottles, diapers, clothes, bibs, blankies, socks, and a framed photo of his most recent ultrasound.

My hand found my parted lips, but it did nothing to stop the whimpers that came from it.

"Oh, honey. I didn't mean to make you cry." My mom rushed toward me and embraced me as best she could with the giant bump between us.

An alien sensation gushed between my legs, and I could feel wetness soaking through my leggings.

"M-Mom." My eyes went wide.

She pulled back, hearing my concern. "What's wrong?"

I couldn't find the words, my fear overwhelming me. I just looked down, my mouth hanging open.

She squinted her eyes and then reached out and touched my leg, feeling the moisture that had saturated my black leggings. "Oh! Oh my gosh. Okay. I'll grab the go bag, and you get in the car." She turned and then spun back around with her finger in the air. "You change. I'll grab the bag, and then we'll go. Time to meet little Jack."

She reached out and kissed my forehead, and I remained frozen.

She took a step to turn and noticed I hadn't moved. "Laura, what are you doing? We've got to go."

My breathing quickened, and my heart rate was skyrocketing. "Mom … Mom, I can't do this. I can't have a baby. I'm not ready. I—"

She grabbed my face in her hands, pulling all of my attention to her. "You listen to me. You are so strong, Laura. No one ever feels ready when this moment comes—no one. It's scary—you're bringing life into this world. But you are ready, baby. I have watched you grow into an incredible woman these last nine months, and that little boy is going to have the best mother anyone could ask for. We don't have time to prepare for the greatest moments; they just simply find us when we need them most."

I nodded, my nerves still eating me alive, but her words began to sink in.

She took my hand in hers, and eighteen hours later, I got to kiss my baby boy for the first time.

I slam my car into park and fly out of it, speed-walking into the building, my hands needing to feel hers again. I nod and smile, going through the motions that I have become so accustomed to with the staff. But they must have had a bad day because they all look sadder than normal.

I smash the elevator button once inside and take a quick ride to her floor.

Once the doors open, my muscles guide me to her room, purely from memory. But when I turn the handle on her door and push it open, the room is empty. And it's not just my mom that's missing. All of the flowers, all of the cards, the pictures Jack colored for her, everything, it's all gone.

I turn around to head to the nurses' station to ask where she was moved when I spot Angie, and a sense of warmth settles into me.

But it fades as fast as it came. Because Angie isn't her usual bubbly self as she's walking my way, slightly behind Dr. Mercer—one of my mom's doctors. She doesn't have a smile plastered across her face. She has her hands locked together in front of her. And she's struggling to meet my eyes.

She opens her mouth, and when she speaks, the six words I hoped I would never hear fall from her lips, and I feel the cold rush of all color draining from my face. "Can we go somewhere to talk?"

My mind blocks out the reason why I'm following Dr. Mercer and Angie into an empty conference room. The what-ifs try to break through my walls, but they don't stand a chance against the denial that is keeping me on my feet.

"Right in here." Dr. Mercer's soft voice pulls me into the room. "Please, take a seat."

My body responds to his words without thought. I can't take my eyes off of him, begging him to tell me everything's okay and that this is just another long talk about my bills and how to handle them.

Angie sits beside me, and I instinctively reach out and take her hand, trying to brace for the impact.

I've never been a big person when it comes to religion, but I send a prayer to every and any god that will listen to not let this be what I think it is.

Dr. Mercer clears his throat. "Late last night, your mother had another stroke. Her heart stopped, in turn stopping blood from pumping to her brain and other organs." He hesitates and takes a deep breath. "We did everything we could. I'm sorry, Laura. Your mother passed away last night."

The breath I just inhaled stalls, sitting midway in my chest. Buzzing sounds in my ears, and my eyes slam shut.

My heart bleeds into my word. "*Please.*"

Dr. Mercer shakes his head. "I'm sorry, Laura. Please take as much time as you need."

I don't fully feel it yet. I don't think my brain will allow me to. I think the pain building in my chest might actually kill me.

But as the door clicks shut behind him, my brain shuts off, and there is no wall stopping the soul-shattering agony from ripping through my body.

I just saw her. I *just* saw her. She was alive and *right there*. I was holding her hand and telling her about Alec and—

It hits me.

The missed phone call last night.

It wasn't about the bills.

It was them calling me about my mom.

And I just ignored it. I ignored it!

What if I would have been able to say goodbye and I missed it?

It's too much.

Regret, anger, love, agony. It's all fighting to take the top spot and I can't take it anymore. I can't.

Images flood my mind.

My mom brushing my hair before bed when I was young. When she showed up at my school and surprised me with my first dog and everyone was so jealous. When I told her I was pregnant and she didn't even miss a beat and went right into planning mode. When my water broke and she helped me bring Jack into the world. When she held him for the first time—I didn't think that I could feel any more love than I did at that moment.

My mind bounces to her stroke. When she didn't wake up. When I realized the last thing I'd said to her wasn't *I love you*.

To bringing Jack to see his grandma in the hospital bed for the first time. To lying in her hospital bed with her and wrapping her arm around me, pretending we were back in our old house and I had just climbed into her bed.

To right now, knowing I will never get to see her beautiful eyes again, never get to feel her put her hand on my shoulder when life gets to be too much. I'll never get to feel her arms wrap around mine. I'll never get to have her walk me down the aisle or go wedding-dress shopping.

And Jack.

Jack will never get all the moments I was already so lucky to have with her.

Everything.

Inside.

Of.

Me.

Breaks.

The first tear rolls down my cheek—a sign of the storm that's about to explode out of me.

I kick my chair back, throwing it against the wall. A guttural scream rips out of me as I back up until I feel the coolness of the wall against my thin shirt.

I fumble for my phone and scroll to Alec's number. I need him. I need him so much right now.

Right as I'm about to press it, Char's picture appears on my screen.

I slide to answer as my last scream rips through the room, and her cheery voice greets me. "Hey, Laura. What're you doing?"

I open my mouth to speak, but nothing comes out.

When Char speaks again, her voice is quiet. "Laura?"

Summoning every ounce of strength I have left, I get two words out, thick with my tears. "She's gone."

"Oh my God. Laura, take a deep breath, honey. I am so sorry. I'm grabbing my keys. I'm coming. We're all coming right now."

Charlotte's always been there, even when I didn't know I needed it. So has Josh. And now, they are all I have left in this world.

She's gone, she's really gone.

Loneliness settles into every cell in my body, and to be honest, I don't know that this feeling will ever leave me.

The next two days are full of, "I'm sorry for your loss," and, "I'm here if you need me."

When people say that, I wonder if they actually mean it or if they say it just to make themselves feel less awkward.

Charlotte took care of all the funeral arrangements and left me and Jack to mourn peacefully in my room instead of picking casket liners and flowers.

I owe her more than she could ever know.

When Char picked me up from the hospital, she had Josh and Jack with her. Josh drove my car home and took Jack for ice cream, so I had time to figure out how to tell him.

And I told him the truth. That Grandma was sick and they couldn't fix her. He asked a thousand questions, which I'd fully expected. And I answered each one as best I could.

We went through old photo albums, through all of the photos on my phone and laptop, and I showed him all the pictures of Mom and me through the years. We had looked through them before, but it felt much different now.

These pictures are truly moments frozen in time. Moments I will never get more of.

The last memory I will have with my mom will involve lowering her in the ground. Part of me wishes this were something I could skip, something I didn't have to be a part of.

But I know that no matter how desperately I don't want to feel that pain, that pain needs to be felt for it to leave me.

At least the pain will be sooner than later. I slip my black panty-hosed feet into my booties and grab my black trench to go with the rest of my black attire.

I opted out of any ounce of makeup, knowing it will be sliding down my face before we even arrive at the church.

I might not have been very religious, but my mom was. She believed we all had a purpose and a path that would find us. But she didn't force it on me. She said that when the time came, it would find me.

I grab my phone and walk to Jack's room, where he is tying his tie around his neck, like he does to his shoelaces. I drop to my knees in front of him, stifling a laugh that rises in my throat. Guilt washes over me that a laugh could even form at all.

"Here, buddy, it's like this." I undo his knot and retie the only tie he owns.

Charlotte picked everything up for us while Josh has been keeping the house clean and keeping us fed and alive.

"Mommy?" his quiet voice asks.

I meet his saddened gaze.

"What will happen to Grandma today?"

I grab his shoulders and pull him down with me as we sit on the floor. "Grandma is going to get a new home, a place in the earth, where we can always go to visit her. To talk to her, tell her about our day, the good and the bad, just like we did in the hospital."

His eyes drift to the side in thought, and then he says, "Can we go see her tomorrow too?"

I nod. "Of course."

I take his little hand in mine and guide us down the stairs, where Charlotte and Josh are waiting. Without a word, we get into the car and drive through the rain to say a final good-bye to the best mom in the world.

Charlotte kept the ceremony small when planning; she knew I wouldn't want a ton of people around. But once my mom's name hit the paper, people all over town wanted to be able to attend, to mourn. And who am I to say they aren't allowed?

When we pull up to the church, a line of people are working their way inside. I take a deep breath in, the air catching in my throat every other second.

Josh parks the car, and I beg my body to stop. To not go inside, to just pretend this isn't real. That she isn't really gone.

But I can't do that to Jack, I can't do that to myself, and I can't do that to her.

When we get out of the car, Jack reaches for my hand, giving it a little squeeze. That's my boy, always looking out for me.

On our way in, everyone offers sad smiles, followed by the phrases you'd expect.

"I'm so sorry."

"She was such a wonderful woman."

"She will be missed."

It continues, even after we take our seats in the front pew. And the tears haven't stopped streaming down my face since we arrived.

The pastor takes the podium, silence greeting him. Silence should be calming, peaceful. But it's not. In the silence, all I hear is her voice, her laugh, her cry. The silence is in the moments that have passed and the ones we'll never see. The silence is eating me alive.

My breaths quicken as he gives an opening prayer.

Breathe. I try to calm myself, but nothing's working. And the spiraling pressure in my chest and lungs is tightening.

I need air. I need fresh air.

I'm on my feet before I know it, barreling down the aisle to the doors. Not a word is said as I burst through them into the pouring rain.

I lift my head up, letting the water blend with the wetness already on my cheeks. The coldness is refreshing and numbing at the same time.

Each drop that hits my face brings me a little closer to calm. And by the time my breathing is normal, I'm drenched head to toe.

I turn and place my hands on the banister of the stairs. But not before something catches my eye.

Not something, but someone.

And not just anyone.

I take my first step off the stairs and run as fast as I can.

And I don't stop until Alec's arms are around me, and the closest thing I've felt to peace in days settles into my chest.

H ome.
My home.

I breathe him in, and his arms tighten around me. After engulfing myself in his embrace for what feels like minutes, I pull back.

And that's when I notice he's not alone. Cam stands to his right and Reed to his left. And my heart feels warmth at the support they're giving me even though we've only known each other for a short time.

They're all dressed head to toe in the finest suits, which now definitely need to go to the dry cleaners.

I offer their saddened eyes a soft smile. "Thank you guys for coming."

My eyes slowly drift back to Alec. Dark circles surround his eyes, and my heart twists for the pain I've caused him.

I want to say something to him, anything. But I can't get any words out.

My mouth opens and closes over and over as tears flood down my cheeks, and my head shakes back and forth, until he takes a step closer to me, his hands falling gently to my arms.

His hazel eyes meet mine, and I swallow the lump in my throat. "You don't have to say a single word right now, Laura. Let's go back inside."

My head involuntarily shakes; I'm afraid that I'm going to spiral again and run.

His right hand glides down my arm and interlocks with my fingers, the raindrops following his touch. "I know it's hard, Lu. I know. But I'm guessing Jack is in there, scared of where you went, and you need to be there for him."

I sigh. He's always known what to say to me, just the right thing. I nod my head, and he leads me inside to face the biggest heartbreak I'll ever know, his hand locked with mine, our hearts reaching to intertwine.

When we get back inside the church, Jack jumps right into Alec's arms, in a similar fashion as I did.

The funeral service is … hard. Seeing her face the same way I did for months feels like we are still in the hospital and I am just waiting for her to wake up. But she's never going to open her eyes again, and I think it will be a long time before I'm willing to accept it.

My mind is empty the rest of the service. I feel like I should be crying harder, having more emotion. But nothing can break through. I think I might have already used my lifetime supply of tears.

Alec offers to give Jack and me a ride home, which we accept. Cam and Reed ride with Char and Josh, who are happy to oblige.

The short ride back to the house is ridden in silence, so many unsaid words hanging in the air between our lips.

When we pull into the driveway, the only thought on my mind is my bed. But the only thought on my heart is Alec. I haven't decided if I have the strength to send him away again. And I'm starting to think he deserves the respect of a choice.

Jack's saddened face smiles at me as we walk inside. Everyone else beat us here, and Char walks straight to Jack when we reach the living room. She knows Alec and I need to talk. And I'm so thankful for her ability to read my mind.

Jack stretches his arms out and lets Char pick him up and carry him to the living room. I hear her offer him ice cream and candy as Alec and I ascend the staircase. I don't even have the energy to shoot her a look at her suggested "meal."

Alec closes the door behind him as I sit on the edge of my bed. The floor is his to start. I'm the one who's already done all the damage.

Alec crosses the room and sits down beside me, a good couple of feet between us. The distance doesn't go unnoticed.

He clears his throat. "Laura, we don't have to talk about anything right now if you aren't up for it, okay? Today has been a lot for you and for Jack, and I don't want you to have to worry. I can wait."

My gaze stays homed in on my white knuckles, where my hands are clasped in my lap. "Postponing this conversation isn't going to make me worry less, only more. Especially when you're right there."

Ugh, nothing I wanted to say even came out. I wanted to say, *Your coach threatened to end your career if I didn't leave you, but I love you, and I've never stopped.*

He nods. "Okay. Do you want me to go?"

My eyes shoot to him. "No. Please no."

A gleam of hope sparkles in his eyes. "Then, I'm not going anywhere."

He lifts his hand off the bed and reaches over to my still-locked fingers. He slowly pulls one away and intertwines our hands.

"Look, Lu, I've been thinking a lot. About me and what I want, about hockey and my future. And I've come to a decision." Alec's voice is definite and concise. I can't tell where he's going with this. "And what I want is right here. I'll have to finish off my contract—I don't have a choice. And I understand it's a lot to ask of you and Jack to deal with my being gone all the time—"

My free hand flics to his mouth and cuts him off. "Stop, Alec. There's something you need to know."

The look of terror that ripples through his features wrecks me.

I remove my hand from his lips and let all the secrets out of mine.

I start at the beginning. "After the game, your coach found me …"

And I continue telling him every detail I can remember. From the coach's conversation to when I called him later that night. And when I went to the hospital and found out about Mom. And by the time I'm done, Alec is fuming.

He's pissed that the coach had the audacity to talk to me like that. And he's livid that I had to go through losing my mom alone. He's in tears within minutes. He's sad that I was forced with that choice. But he couldn't help but smirk when I told him about how I planned to go around the coach.

"I love you. Please, let's find a way to work through this together, not by yourself. You are never alone in this life, Lu, you will have me till the day I die, and even after that."

I'm speechless as anger seems to take back over his features. He's pacing back and forth when there's a knock on the door.

"Mommy?" Jack's little voice calls from the other side of the door.

Alec's shoulders instantly loosen, the anger dissipating quickly.

"Come in," I call to Jack.

The door swings open, and Jack is standing there with a question on his mind, his eyes big and his lips twisted.

"What's up, buddy?" I ask him.

"Um, I heard Dad shouting, and I wanted to make sure you guys were okay." He swings his hands behind his back, rocking on his feet.

Alec sighs and immediately drops to Jack's height, grabbing his small shoulders. "Hey, everything's okay. I was angry but not at your mom. At something else. Everything's perfect, little man."

Jack instantly smiles and turns around without another word. Well, until he gets a few steps away. "I'm getting a cookie! Char said I could have as many as I want today!"

I giggle as I hear his pitter-patter descend the stairs.

Alec walks over, the intensity of our convo resuming, and shuts the door.

I'm hyperaware of his movements. I know he said he wants us to be together, but I'm scared. I broke his heart. And yeah, my intentions were good, and the breakup wasn't real for me, but I still hurt him.

He stops, where I'm sitting on the edge of the bed and kneels before me, his hands sliding to my waist. "Listen to me, Laura. Hockey has been my life since I was two years old, maybe even before then. It's given me everything I have now, and for that, I'm grateful. Without it, I might never have run into you again."

His thumbs slide up and down my sides as he gathers his next words.

"But if you think for one second that I wouldn't give it all up to be right here with you and Jack, you, my woman, are batshit crazy."

He laughs, and I can't help the one that slips past my smile.

He continues, "Clumsy, I love you. I've always loved you. That night when I ran into you at Fireflies, I was in shock that you were there, that out of every place in the entire world, you were in the same room as me. You've always been gorgeous, for as long as I've known you. But you are fucking beautiful and sexy, and I wouldn't change a single thing about you. You're the sweetest woman I've ever known, completely selfless. And you're the most amazing mother. You are funny, and kind to everyone you meet. You would sacrifice your own heart in an attempt to save mine. But there was a fatal flaw with your plan. My heart won't survive if it can't love you."

My eyes burn, and tears cloud my vision. But for the first time in days, they're not tears of loss or pain.

He moves closer to me, his lips mere inches from mine. "I know you still have two months of school left, and I know you and Jack have built a life here. And I couldn't be prouder of you."

A flame flickers through his eyes seconds before he leans in and kisses me, his hand sliding around the back of my neck and squeezing. Our kiss is not gentle and clean; it's messy with teeth clashing and tongues dancing, and passion flares.

His cheeks are pink when he pulls back. "Sorry. I just … you were way too close, and it's been way too long."

He smirks and hesitates before he says, "Duluth is a hell of a ways from New York. And I was hoping that when you finish school, I could convince you two to move in with me. I don't want to spend a second more apart from you guys than I already have. Jack will be able to be around the team and continue to pursue hockey if he wants. He'll have the best of the best of everything. And I get the both of you." He bites his lip in anticipation. "What do you say?"

I don't have time to answer before the bedroom door flies open, and Jack tackles us both. "Oh my God! We're moving to New York!"

Alec laughs, and I scowl at Jack for eavesdropping. The tears that roll down my cheeks fall onto my dress, a mixture of the sadness from saying an eternal good-bye and the promise of a happy forever.

SIX MONTHS LATER

"**G**o, Jack!" I shout, throwing my arms in the air. Number 28 passes it to Jack as he skates into the right wing, and two seconds later, he scores the winning goal against the Wolves.

"Woo!" Alec shouts with his arms wrapped around my waist.

The rest of the New York Nighthawks erupt in cheers and hoots for Jack and the Warriors, Jack's hockey team.

Char and Josh couldn't make it; they had to deal with some plumbing issues at their apartment. They don't live in Duluth anymore. They decided to brave the long move to New York. They still live together, and they have a gorgeous apartment in the city. Char found a new club to work at even though Reed insists on paying for everything. Char lets him occasionally but only when she feels the need to be spoiled.

Josh was excited to get out of Duluth. He lit up when Alec and I told him about the move. I think he might have stayed all that time in Duluth just for Charlotte and me.

Jack's team barrels into him, and the coach claps proudly from the bench.

Jack started playing for the Warriors once we moved in with Alec in New York. Jack has never seemed happier. He even has a boyfriend, and his name is Ethan. It must be something about those E named boys. I laugh to myself.

Ethan is sitting next to Alec, asking all the questions about hockey and how it works. Alec is lapping it up, and I'm so thankful that he has never once made Jack or Ethan feel anything less than acceptance and pride. I turn to look behind me and smile at Ethan's parents, who are lost, watching the game.

Jack introduced us to Ethan at his last parent-teacher conference. Thankfully, Ethan's parents are as supportive of their relationship as we are.

Jack never really came out per say, but he didn't exactly need to. I have always told him that it is okay to love who you love shamelessly. So, when he came home from school and told us all about Ethan, we were thrilled he felt comfortable to share with us fearlessly.

Of course, after the game—and occasionally during—Alec and his teammates get ambushed for autographs and pictures. But that has just become our new normal. After the wave of press, we say our good-bye to Ethan and his parents.

The Nighthawks have been Jack's biggest fans at his games. The new coach has even made it to one. When the owner, Jameson Havemeyer, found out what the old coach had pulled—threatening Alec's professional career over his personal affairs—he was let go. I was impressed.

And now, I get to call Mr. Havemeyer my boss. After I graduated with my bachelor's, Mr. Havemeyer gave me a call, offering me the position of marketing director for the Nighthawks. He said he saw my marketing campaign with The Crooked Spine and was very impressed with my innovation and creativity.

I get to work from my laptop, which is the greatest thing. I have an official office at the arena, but I'm hardly ever in it. Between Alec's schedule, Jack's schedule, and my own, I normally get most of my work done next to the ice.

My flexible schedule also allows us to travel back to Duluth to visit my mom. We are catching a flight today, headed to see her. After his game, we quickly load up and before I know it, we are pulling into the airport.

The driver slows to a stop, and we hurry out, already late for our flight. We grab our luggage and take off running to get through security as fast as possible.

Luckily, the line moves very fast, and before we know it, we are handing our carry-ons to the flight attendants and boarding the plane.

We've traveled back home about once every other month since the move. It's nice for Jack to visit Mom, and I miss her all the time. So, any trip we make never seems like enough. Alec normally distracts Jack enough to give me a few minutes alone with her. We've never used words to communicate this, and we've never needed to. Alec just knows.

This trip will be a quick one; we are only going to be there for the night. Alec's next game is tomorrow night, and we have to get on our flight back at six a.m.

I offered to change our tickets, but Alec wouldn't budge. Even though this seemed like a lot more work for him for no reason. But I gave in and stopped pushing it because I get to visit my mom again.

Thankfully, the flight goes smoothly, and when we land, it's only four o'clock. Plenty of time for dinner and a good visit with Mom.

Alec leads our aisle out of the plane, and we grab our carry-ons as we exit. When we get out of the secured area, a man is waiting with a sign for Kostelecky along with a plethora of paparazzi.

You'd think I'd get used to the drivers and the cameras, but sometimes, it still catches me by surprise that this is our life. We follow the driver to the limo, and when we get inside, Alec pours me a glass of champagne.

"Are we celebrating?" I ask him, taking the glass.

He squints his eyes at me. "Of course. Jack just had the game-winning shot." He fist-bumps Jack.

I reach over and squeeze his knee, pride coursing through me. It wasn't too long ago that he was getting fitted for skates for the very first time.

He's learning so fast, no doubt due to the intense training schedule that Alec and his trainer created. But Jack seems serious. This is what he wants—to play hockey for life. So, we will make sure we give him everything he needs to get there.

A glass, or two, or three later, we are pulling to a stop. The driver opens the door, and I instantly look at him, confusion flooding me.

"Um, sir, this is not the cemetery." I glance back to Alec, who does not seem surprised in the least at our change of destination.

He just smirks and turns to the driver. "Thanks, Tom. Give us twenty."

"Alec, what are you—"

Alec's hand clamps over my mouth. "Shh. For once in your life, no questions."

I roll my eyes at him but give him what he wants. The driver follows Alec's unspoken orders and leads Jack inside to get some food.

When I turn back to Alec, he is pulling something out of his pocket, a folded up envelope.

"Now that we have the same address, I can't really sneak it into your mailbox." He hands me the folded in half envelope and my heart swells.

My cheeks burn as I ask, "Is-is this a letter? Like our old letters?"

He nods. "Read it, please."

I lick my lips and carefully remove the letter and set the envelope on the seat next to me.

Dear Laura,

I have loved you for what feels like my entire life. I fell in love with you when I was sixteen years old.

And I don't know what happened to the last letter you wrote me all those years ago, maybe the mailman stole it, or the mailbox blew open and the wind took it, we'll never know. I wish I could have that time back with you, with Jack. But who knows, maybe we wouldn't be where we are today if I ever got that letter. If I didn't move across the country, I would have watched your stomach grow with Jack inside and I would have known that you were pregnant and I would have convinced you to be with me again. There are so many what if's that have run through my mind.

But I don't care about what if's anymore, Lu, because we're together again and that's all that matters to me. I get to watch Jack grow and fall in love with hockey. I get to watch him love you, I get to see how he looks at you when you don't even know he's watching. I get to hold you in my arms every single night, I get to love you every single day. We may have lost some time together early on, but I choose to be with you, to love you every day. And that will never change, my love for you will never waiver. Because, Lu, I fell for you the day you were pushed off those steps and into my arms, and I've never stopped.

I love you when you're sad, when you're mad, when you're scared. I love you when you love Jack. I love you when you love me. I love you in the hot summer days. I love you in every scenario, in every way.

And I will love you, even in the storm and even in the rain.

Tears roll down my cheek as I fold the letter up and set it on top of the envelope.

My love for him swells in my chest and I throw my arms around him, squeezing as hard as I can.

With my face pressed into his chest, I say, "I love you."

His hands grab my waist and he pulls me into his lap, "I love you too, Clumsy."

I adjust in his lap and he pushes his hips up, rolling against me.

I smirk, "Well, you said twenty-minutes right? We have to have at least fifteen of that left."

Alec looks at me with a look in his eyes that I have come to know oh-so well. His hand fists into my hair and he pulls me to him as our lips crash together.

He pulls away just to watch my lips part as he slides my skirt up my legs, a devilish smile dancing on his full lips.

"Laura Young, what am I going to do with you?" Alec teases as his lips and tongue find that sweet spot on the base of my neck.

Alec's fingers graze my entrance and then quickly slip inside, taking me by surprise. He begins pumping in and out furiously, and my hands grip the seat tight to keep my hips from bucking.

Alec pulls his torturous kiss from my neck, and with his free hand, he turns my face to his, our lips inches apart. "You are so wet and ready for me."

His fingertips lift up, hitting all new nerves inside me.

"Always." The word falls breathlessly and desperately out of my mouth.

"Good girl." Alec's fingers pull out, and in one swift movement, I'm straddling his lap, holding myself up by his shoulders.

He hastily undoes his belt and shimmies his pants down past his rock-hard erection.

I lick my lips at the sight, craving to feel him again.

He lines his tip up with my entrance and with impeccable control, his hands grab my hips, and he slowly lowers me onto him, gradually filling me inch by inch.

Alec's voice is deep and chock-full of unbridled need as he asks, "Are you ready?"

He throbs inside me, and I moan, "Yes. Please yes."

His hands on my hips lift me up slightly, allowing a few inches of space between us with his full erection still inside me.

The anticipation builds when he doesn't immediately take control.

Alec's voice calls to every cell in my body. "Look at me and don't ever stop."

And with that, his control snaps. His hands slam my hips down, and he lifts me back up. But this time, he doesn't pull me down; he thrusts up.

And with each thrust, he gets harder and faster. Within minutes, I'm close to the edge, and as my name drifts from his panting lips, we dive into pleasure together.

After a few moments of calm and coming back to reality, Alec says, "Come on. I have something to show you."

I let him take my hand and lead me around Al's Barbecue to the small pond we grew up skating on. The pond where we shared our first kiss.

We round the corner, and two pairs of skates sit on the bench on the edge of the frozen pond.

Alec grabs the smaller pair and hands them to me. "Here, put these on."

I hesitate wondering where in the hell these came from. But Alec seems to always have a trick up his sleeve. So I don't say a word as I grab the skates and quickly lace up. Alec does the same.

"You ready?" he asks, offering me his hand.

I accept it, and we glide onto the ice, skating hand in hand. Just like we did years ago.

"Do you remember the first time we came here?" he asks, twirling me under his arm.

My heart warms at the memory of one of our first dates. "Of course. It was great until we raced, and I fell and broke my ass."

He laughs. "You didn't actually break your ass."

"Well, it felt like I did." I nudge his arm, skating into him.

He reciprocates. "Okay, well, now that you're basically a pro, let's try again."

He turns around and finds his place next to me.

Competition ignites in my veins. I know I won't beat him, but I might be able to trip him and win. I laugh to myself at my scheming tactics.

Alec grabs my hand and spins me around, pulling me against his chest. His fingers brush my hair out of my face, and my heart skips a beat as he leans down and kisses me.

"Not fair!" I shout at him, knowing he's just trying to fluster me. I retake my spot by his side.

"You ready? From here to the edge." He nods across the small pond.

I crack my neck. "Ready."

He counts down. "Three, two, one, *go!*"

I take off, digging the blades into the ice. He's in my peripheral vision, but I think I'm slightly ahead. Only five more feet to go.

I drop my focus on Alec and give the last few feet everything I have before quickly stopping, reaching the edge.

Holy shit, I won!

I spin around to rub it in his face, and all air huffs out of my lungs. My hands fly to my mouth, which has dropped open. And my eyes become blurry from the tears welling as I look down to Alec on one knee with a black velvet box in his hand.

His smile is so big as he speaks, emotion thick in his voice. "Laura, the first day I brought you to this pond, I told myself, *I'm going to marry that girl one day.* We got lost somewhere along the way, but you were brought back to me with the best gift the universe could have ever given me—Jack. Through a lost letter and years apart, I never stopped loving you. That day that I saw you at Fireflies, I vowed I wouldn't let you go again. And I will uphold that vow for the rest of our lives. There has never been anyone other than you, Lu."

He lifts the lid of the box, showing an elegant ring with one large diamond and a plain platinum band. "Will you marry me?"

Nothing could have prepared me for the heartache I faced this last year. And nothing could have prepared me for the love that I found again. But that's the beauty of life. It's messy, and it's hard, but if you have someone special by your side, nothing else matters.

I fall to my knees, taking Alec's hands in mine. "Of course. Of course I'll marry you."

He takes the ring out of the box and slides it onto my left ring finger, and it's a perfect fit.

He throws the velvet box on the ice and grabs my face, his hands sliding around my jaw. He brings my lips to his, sealing our fate.

All of a sudden, I hear cheers coming toward us. I turn and see Charlotte, Josh, and Jack carefully running our way.

Plumbing issues, my ass. I laugh.

They slide into us, wrapping their arms around us. And in that moment, I feel like I just scored the game-winning shot.

A raindrop hits my cheek, and I look up just in time to see the sky split, rain pouring down on us.

And in that moment, I can't help but think, *Those are my mom's tears of joy, her way of letting us know she's right here. She always has been and always will be.*

Author's Notes

Alec and Laura's story is special to me. I have had these characters in my head and my heart since I was sixteen years old. Being able to bring them to life has been an incredible journey, and I'm so excited to watch them grow through the course of this stand-alone series.

Loss of a loved one is something that I am sure we have all experienced. It is never easy, and every day is hard. I hope this book helped you feel less alone in your healing, knowing that sometimes, even when we can't hold ourselves up, we all have someone who will.

LGBTQIA+ is also a topic I touched on with Jack, and one that I am passionate about. I believe that anyone should be able to love who they want. And who are we to stop someone else from being happy? Children know who they are, no matter what outside forces influence them. Love is love, and no one can help who they fall in love with. I myself have always struggled to accept my sexuality. I have been in a relationship with the love of my life since I was sixteen years old. But that doesn't change my sexuality. I would be open to loving any gender and any sexual orientation, and I always have been. But until recently, I never let myself acknowledge it, in fear of being rejected or unloved. But I cannot hope to help inspire others to be themselves if I cannot do the same for myself. I hope that you can live being fearlessly you. If you ever need someone to talk to, if you need someone to support you for simply being you, I will always be your hype girl. Message me on instagram and I will send you all the love and support. Because I love you just the way you are, you are strong, beautiful, brilliant, and I am so proud of the person you are right now. I hope that Jack can give you inspiration to live and love the way you want without boundaries. To be you, because you fucking rock.

ACKNOWLEDGMENTS

Thank you, reader, for picking up *Find Me in the Rain*. Without you, this story would just be words on a page. Your imagination and time bring them to life, and for that, I am forever grateful. You help me live out my dreams every single day, and I owe you everything.

Nikki, I love you, and I would not be where I am without you. You push me to keep writing when I hit roadblocks. You send books to my house for inspiration. The hours and hours we spend on FaceTime, writing together, are some of my most cherished memories. Even though we live states away from each other, you are my best friend, and you are the soul mine has always been searching for. Oh, and I haven't forgotten that you still might be a serial killer and just haven't killed me yet.

Dante, thank you for always having unwavering faith in me in all aspects of my life. Thank you for believing in my writing and always supporting me. You are my inspiration for the love in my books, and I would be truly lost without you by my side. I love you forever and always.

Jovana, my editor, thank you for putting up with my never-ending emails and the ones yet to come. I owe you my sanity, because. I would be lost without your help! You are incredible and I am so grateful for all the time you put into my books. And thank you for taking the jumble of words I send you and turning them into a novel. You are magic.

My parents, brother, and family, thank you for always choosing to see the best in me, and thank you for believing in me. Without your never-ending support, I don't know that I would have the courage to write, to spill my heart onto these pages. Thank you for loving me for me.

To me.

Is that weird? Oh well.

To me, for following my crazy, wild stories that have lived in my head for years and putting them down on paper. Without the characters and voices talking in my head, this would never exist. And I've never been prouder to be a little crazy.

To all the wine and French fries that helped me write this book, you are the real hero that brought it to life.

Oh! And to the people who didn't believe in me and thought I would amount to nothing, I hope both sides of your pillow are hot when you go to bed tonight.

Printed in Great Britain
by Amazon